Carving Elsewhere

by

Keith D. Jacobs

Grey Lodge Press
USA

Carving Elsewhere by Keith D. Jacobs
Copyright © 2024 Keith D. Jacobs

ISBN: 979-8-9912302-3-0 (Paperback)

Library of Congress Control Number (LCCN): 2024915882

Cover Illustration by Racheal Bruce.
Interior Illustrations by Marty Chapelle.

Printed in the United States of America.

First Printing Edition 2024.

Grey Lodge Press
greylodgepress@gmail.com

To my father,

who always encouraged me to
write a book about my world travels.

...instead, I wrote this.
Sorry.

With fire in your eyes, may it never go out
    The sweetness of your tears make it feel like night
I see no escape from the roles we always play
    What do we have to prove on this judgement day?

— Oingo Boingo

CARVING ELSEWHERE

I have found solace in the knife. A sharp one.

Lately, I have been thinking about my time at college. If I had stayed there and graduated would I find myself in a different place, both my station in life and my mental position in the present day to day? Would I still be learning by the book? Attempting to be more social and craving the attention of girls I could have made more of an effort with? Finding comfort in being young and thinking I had all the time on earth to follow through with whatever daydreams that sparked. Would I be here, in the New England wilderness or back in Mississippi with my Ole Miss classmates? Would I still come to this point at my age and find solace in a sharp knife?

PROLOGUE

The drive up from Mississippi went smooth by most standards of a long distance trip. Normally, I will enjoy music while I am in a car by myself. Instead, I spent almost the entirety of this drive reflecting on what I left and the life I was heading to. My mind stirred with dark lonesome impulses that I only then figured out on the drive were not entirely normal for most people. Fantasies of living alone. My own little plot of land with a modest little cabin. Where I can work on maybe writing stories and even music. Creating art and sculptures. Possibly bringing someone to the isolation I created and making them a part of it in a horrific way, against their will.

I made the trip in just two days of driving a ragged twenty-year-old Chevy pickup. This nineteen seventy-seven truck was probably blue when it was built but now more of a despicable faded grey. The down-on-his-luck old man who sold me the vehicle seemed to really have a bond with it. You can tell he cherished it. Regardless, I had no problem offering him well below what he asked, which was already well below what it was worth. He clearly took good care of the truck and despite its outward appearance, due probably only to time and use conditions, it was solid all around, internally and otherwise. If he had painted it before selling he surely could have gotten double what he was asking for; if he had time to let it sit in the classifieds a bit longer, that is. Luckily for me, his divorce finances, after forty years of marriage, did not allow for time or a new coat of paint.

I stopped to rest somewhere in Ohio on the first night of driving. Pulled the truck down a small dirt road and parked snug up to some large bushes where I figured no one would bother me. An hour before finding this spot I filled up the gas tank, so there would be no need to worry about it in the morning before hitting the road again. At the gas station was this loud, obnoxious middle aged man arguing on the payphone. His car was parked at the pump directly in front of mine. Seeing as my gas tank was nearly empty I spent a long, dragged out fill-up listening to this idiot yell about his unwillingness to stop at the post office on his way home. Safe to assume, this was his wife or girlfriend on the phone. He sounded completely irrational and vindictive about the situation. Apparently he has the keys to their postal box and went on telling the person on the other end that she never makes an effort to do things for him. He brought up things that did not seemingly apply to the situation at hand. Even going so far as to mention things about her past relationships and people she had slept with, culminating into him calling her a few vulgar names.

I was annoyed enough to catch up with this man down the dark highway and flash my lights at him. He pulled over and did not seem to recognize me from the gas station when I approached his car.

I tell him, "There's sparks flying from underneath your vehicle."

He looked back as if he actually expected to see sparks now that the car was stopped.

I add, "Must be dragging a bit of metal, that'd be my guess."

This is, of course, a lie. He steps out with clear worriment and we walk back to inspect the problem. He turns a small pocket flashlight on and bends down with full concentration. Oblivious. Before he makes it all the way down to a proper crouch I slip the small L-shaped tire iron out from my right-hand sleeve and quickly grab it with my left hand. All in one motion I strike him right where the neck ends and the back of his head begins. He drops to the ground, as expected, but unexpectedly without a sound. I could not believe, in all of my experience with hearing this loudmouth idiot, that this was the one time he did not make a peep.

I look at the man faced down on the ground for a few seconds, surely trying to figure out the confusion of his current pain. It only takes those few seconds for me to realize that I would like to strike him several more times. A few more blows to his back and he is totally laid out. I almost think that I heard a bone crack, possibly a back rib or two. My next move is to stomp on a stretched hand he uses to reach out with, having no sure reason why I did this. Could be because it was the hand he used to hold the phone, a conduit for my annoyance earlier. Now I take his keys from him, leaving him hurt and relatively stranded.

In the long run, I think this will bring him and his partner closer together. I was not considering this at first, but as I left I was certain that this situation would lead to these two appreciating each other more. I think about him not coming home. She will wait up for him, completely worried. Her head will go all sorts of places and wonder if the fight they just had on the phone made him decide not to come home tonight. Did he go to a hotel, and if so, did he find a bar to drink this anxiety away? Did he meet someone there? Or, is it possible he got into an accident? This thought will likely be worse than the others in her mind. Because if he is seriously injured in a car wreck she will feel like the direct cause for rattling his cage about the mail. Whichever way it goes, he will not be home in time anywhere near expected. She will drive herself crazy and completely erase any frustration concerning him about the mail and argument and even the nasty things he called her.

As for the man, the sorry excuse for a partner regarding his recent attitude, someone will find him here. Most likely unconscious. They will immediately call the police, ambulance and their own friends and family to brag about the whole thing and give themselves a pat on the back for being a savior. The injured man will wake up in an ambulance or hospital and eventually see the loving, caring face of his partner. Her face will show total unconditional love, forgiveness and forgetness of any contemptible problem they have ever had. He will see her and immediately realize what he has and it will be his wakeup call to treat her better, or some kind of stupid sentiment like this that movies convince us to regurgitate. Maybe this awakening that they both have will last and maybe it will not. This is all out of my control. I can only help them so much.

The next morning I woke up in my sleeping bag inside the covered bed of my truck. I slept the whole night through, mostly undisturbed. The weather was just cool enough to warrant a sleeping bag. Perfect camping weather in my opinion. If I can sleep all night without being too cold or too hot at any point then I have got an ideal camping situation. I give myself a good long, eyes-closed stretch while still snug in my plaid flannel cocoon. This is all it takes to be completely energized and get up, roll the sleeping bag and then throw it to the passengers side as I climb into the driver's seat. I opened the large bubble-protected envelope that I picked up from the obnoxious man's post office box last night. The long driving session from the previous day had me so tired that I decided I would not appreciate these spoils until fully rested.

I ripped the top of the package and dumped the contents out onto my lap. The items inside are nothing special. A few used books, mostly new titles I have never heard of. Before I drove off to continue my journey to the northeast I leaned over and rolled down the passenger side window to throw the books out. All except one. A blank notebook that I could use to write things down in.

I start to wonder if I tend to over-explain things. Something to hopefully work on as I continue to fill the journal. That and the bitter viewpoints I am regularly prone to.

The drive this day is just as straightforward as the day before. I zone out with my thoughts and before I know it I am in a random northwest Massachusetts town called Saint Ox. Choosing this region was somewhat premeditated because I have heard that cheap land, often with homes on them already, is in abundance. I do not have much money by most standards, but at the same time, I have enough to get by and the ingenuity to make more. Hopefully it is at least enough to purchase a small starter property for myself. For many reasons, this has become a truly important goal for me. Owning something fully and not having to pay someone else rent or crash freely on another person's couch is the most befitting move that someone like me can make. Full control of my own space is a core determination.

I park the truck downtown and pop a few quarters into the parking meter. The people around town give a few looks as I turn from the street to walk down the sidewalk. I believe this is because of the Mississippi plates. It could not be because of my truck's appearances as there are plenty around that have the same aesthetic. And not because of my own appearance because I am indistinguishable from everyone I see, maybe just a bit more tired-looking. Sure enough, an older lady in business attire comes out of a pizza shop holding a slice on a paper plate, just a few doors down from where I parked. She tells me she saw me pull up from inside and tries to ask me about Mississippi and what brings me up here. This seems genuine and not at all intrusive as she inquires, but I am not in the mood for small talk. I give her just enough conversation and lay on a southern accent while doing so. This is not my natural dialect as I am not even from the south.

"All the way from Mississippi? What brings you up to our neck of the woods?" she asks, seemingly earnest, with a dumb inquisitive half-smile on her face.

I am caught off guard when I notice how exquisite her piercing green eyes are. True green eyes like these, as I have learned from my biology courses, are exceedingly rare.

"Well now, I sure always dreamed of bein' more refined an' New England seems 'bout the classiest place I can learn to be just that," I say, in a totally condescending manner, but she does not pick up on this as I am presenting myself as completely serious.

"Well good for you for wanting to better yourself. So what's it like in Mississippi?"

I find this response should be a little bit offensive and the question itself is way too broad to award an answer. Small talk with no substance or of wanting to actually know the answer. She engaged me purely out of novelty in talking to an outsider, someone from far away. I believe this woman might actually have some questions for me deep down, but until she refines herself I am certain that I have no need for this useless back and forth. In fact, I am becoming annoyed to the point of wanting to lash out at her.

I tell her, "Well ma'am, Mississippi is a lot like what you think."

I leave it at that and wonder what she actually perceives about me and the place I came from. The statement hangs for a second. I am sure she thought I would finish that thought with some southern wit, but I do not. I stare at her as she attempts to bring the slice of pizza up to her face. She then realizes I am done talking and it is her turn. The slice gets lowered back down on the soggy paper plate and she remains unsatisfied with not being able to take the bite. I hold and deepen my stare so she knows she absolutely has to say something now.

With a slightly flustered air, she musters up, "I'm sure it's lovely."

Internally, I am extremely irritated now. I was hoping for some entertainment in her response, but she gave me nothing. I suppose I expected too much. But I am determined to leave this exchange with something of value to me. So I ask about any available property in the area. This is clearly a woman who is outgoing enough to probably know everyone in town. Her usefulness might actually reveal itself in this moment.

"The old Mitchell house. Peter and Sue moved down to Florida for retirement. Mary Webb, a newly widowed native of the area, moved herself into a new house across town and her old one is up for grabs. Saint Ox has many options at the moment."

She listed five more homes before I interjected and asked about potential properties further outside of town. Apparently, there is a ton of land up for sale but most are all way out in the middle of nowhere; forestland and mountains that go on forever. She tells me this as if these are not my ideal specifications for somewhere to live; being far away from everything.

I am not completely unsatisfied with our exchange anymore. There is now more than a hint of promise in this area which may lead to securing a bit of property for myself. With that, I start to devise some plans to hunt for what I want.

PART ONE

-1-

Over the next few days I drive out in all directions from Saint
Ox exploring the vast wilderness. There are plenty of long-
forgotten, unused and overgrown dirt roads that get me to where
I want to go. And when those roads end, I haul my truck
through the untraversed parts of the forest, making my own
paths.

One evening, about forty-five minutes outside of town
and further up into the Berkshire Mountains wilderness, I start
to feel tired and discouraged from the failures of the past few
days. Knowing that the sun is going down, and that I still have
not found a piece of property for myself, it would be unwise to
start the drive back towards Saint Ox. So I decide to search for a
place to sleep in the area I am currently in.

Finding a proper spot to camp for the night is an
important skill. Of course, when you are on the road and racing
to get somewhere you take the first convenient place; rest stop,
parking lot of a major superstore, abandoned backroad. But
when you have nowhere to be you have options. The perfect
comfortable spot is now something to consider.

At long last, scouting this region with what little light I have left I think I have found it. It is not so heavily condensed with trees, oddly enough, compared to the rest of the area that I have seen so far. I have room to breathe a little bit. Brown autumn leaves coat the forest floor and it feels like a crunchy, yet slick rug as I take a short walk in my socks to urinate. Then I head back to climb into the truck bed.

My comfort is maxed. Both physically and mentally. Most of the time, when I camp out, there is always someone nearby. This is obvious in places like parking lots and highway pull-offs, but even at campgrounds where the idea is to get away from it all. Sure, designated camping areas take you out of town and into nature, but there are always people around out there as well. With a busy mind like mine I can always find a reason to be annoyed when others are around, seen or unseen. Even if I can slightly make out minor traces of voices, then I am completely engulfed in it as a distraction. I will end up doing something like yelling at someone angrily or nearly burning the tongues off of two college kids with white-hot coals from their campfire. An incident I could not stick around for to see their final condition. For them, this was probably the worst experience of firsthand chaos they have ever known; their finest example of human entropy. Now, even if there is no one around at all I still get the unpleasant expectation that someone will pull up during the night and break my comfort spell. Whether anyone shows up or not is inconsequential. The seed is unpleasantly planted by default and my dread of being potentially bothered is practically the same as actually being bothered. A reasonable person might ask themselves why someone like me even goes out or if I could ever truly be comfortable at all? The answer is yes, I can be and the proof is happening this very moment.

This spot has got a relaxing hold on me. I cannot wait to see what morning looks like when the sunlight comes poking through this clearing I have found. For a fleeting moment, as I lay in my sleeping bag staring through the window of my truck shell up at the trees and open gaps between them to view the stars, I think about the business woman I spoke with when I arrived in Saint Ox. An unexplainable aggravation fills me as I run through all the little details that made this person up. The way she approached me, her dense questions, all the doltish looks she wore, the sound of her voice and the way she used it. Once I get to thinking about things like this it is hard to snap myself out of it. I struggle in forcing myself to shift my mental brooding back to a comfortable state. To where I am now, in this exact moment.

Before too long, I am sound asleep.

-2-

The dark crimson morning bled through the trees and over me like a lion's soaked face as he pulls it out of a fresh, partially eaten, kill. Totally relaxed and comfortable with what is happening after the hyper-focused thrill of a hunt. Though, my hunt was less messy and specifically for a nearly perfect location rather than a food source, as far as anyone else is concerned. I guess you could also say that there was another hunt. Allegedly, this was only in my mind, after the encounter with the woman leaving the pizza shop. When she walked away

I took a moment to imagine what it would be like to follow her
home. Then wondered what her head would look like without
eyes. Or a body.

I allow myself a good long stretch before shaking off
the sleep and hopping out of the truck to explore the area better.
First thing I realized was how far out and away I was from
anywhere and anyone. It really sank into me that I was further
than I had perceived yesterday evening. It also became more
evident that no one has been around here in ages. Years and
years upon years.

I picked a direction in this massive remoteness and
started walking. It felt good knowing I did not have to drive all
day today and I took full advantage of this by wandering around
on foot. There was something in the near distance that caught
my attention. It was big and dark and filled me with wonder just
from the far away view I had. This feeling that is rushing up
was one I did not know I had lost and missed for so long. It
reminds me of back when I was a young boy. I used to go out
and explore places the way I am now, with such excitement of
not knowing what I would find around every corner. There
would be this sort of curious bewilderment about getting to
experience something new, as if it were giving me some kind of
essential life force. As I got older it seems I lost this feeling. I
suppose I still go out and do these things but it is almost as if to
satisfy some urge rather than it coming from a place of real
passion. Have I just been dying inside, little by little, only to
one day be shrunk so much to having no real feelings or
emotions towards anything?

At this moment I feel a great reversal of that curse as I
approach a glorious dark wooded and longtime-abandoned
church. This modest structure was certainly rundown but still
had all the basic components. Four walls, though some wood

panels have been heavily or completely ripped out and most of which could use a cleaning. A couple of little stained glass windows are on each side, with only a few missing pieces all together. And a small spire attached to a steeple pointing up from the front side. Oddly enough, this part of the structure is the most in tact.

I step through the large old wooden doors, which were already a bit open, and am intoxicated at the sight of the simple altar ahead. The floor was almost entirely dirt with nearly none of the wood left. Could be that the rest was buried by all the earth and forest debris that let itself in, but this was not something I spent much time thinking about. Marveling at the sight of all the pews still present and intact, though slightly warped, I proceeded up to the altar. This stage area was raised about knee-height above the rest of the room. It still had the wooden podium to bring the whole place together, not to mention a solid looking stone fireplace against the back wall on the stage. I step up onto the little stool for the podium and look out unto my audience of leaves and branches, animal nests and pieces of roof. The roof was the biggest issue with this church. The gable roof had certainly seen better days. Considerable holes and gaps riddled it so that the outside could easily come through. I kick branches and rubble around as I walk about, optimistic that I may discover some hidden treasure, or at the very least, a relic from this gathering place's former life.

When moving a particularly leafy pile of debris by the wall, at one side of the stage, there is a noticeably warped and loose square-shaped piece of wood flooring that is no bigger than my hand. Upon inspection and removal of the panel I found that I did indeed manifest a treasure. In the heart of this nifty hiding place was an antiquated jar that perhaps held pickles in its former glory. Inside the jar was a glass vial roughly the size of my thumb. I walk myself over to the front row of tottering pews and settle into a cross-legged sit.

The lid of the first jar took some muscle but popped off without breaking the glass, as I feared might happen. The vial inside was capped extremely tight with a cork plug that I wrestle with for just a moment before deciding to hold off until I was ready to use the contents inside. It contained six strips of paper around the size of those pH test strips you see people using to check the chemical balance of their swimming pools. The strips have nine perforated lines going through them, short-ways, to make ten tabs on each strip. Totaling sixty tabs. Clearly this LSD was hidden, left behind and possibly forgotten about. I then validated my choice not to open the vial just yet as exposing the drug to as little oxygen as possible was beneficial in retaining potency, assuming there was any left.

At this time, I study the lid from the presumed pickle jar that contained this little bottle of shining interest. I found it had an expiration date from the early nineteen-seventies. This would make the acid inside nearabout twenty-five years old, or more. Which would also mean it may be pretty strong stuff given the era it was manufactured. The vial was put back in the jar and the jar back into the floor for safe keeping. I spent the rest of this day and all of the next one mostly relaxing and inactive in order to bounce back from the road fatigue accumulated on the drive up from Mississippi.

The ravens perch in trees that surround the church above me. They add a much welcomed menacing vibe to the scene. I can sense a foreboding atmosphere taking root and can feel in my essence the atrocious potential activity this setting has to offer.

3

Navigating my way back from Saint Ox was not exactly simple, even with all the landmarks and mental directions I retained. This is a good thing. I do not want my elsewhere hidden sanctum accessible and effortless to find. With only a few wrong turns, which easily could have left me completely displaced and lost, I was able to catch myself and rediscover my claimed asylum before I had gone too far off track.

All the fundamental provisions were purchased to sustain me for at least a week. For food, it was mostly nonperishable canned and bagged fare like rice, tuna, cereal, beans, bread, peanut butter, quick-cook grits, flour tortillas and oatmeal. I was also sure to fetch an ample amount of fresh produce that should keep if I stay vigilant. Sweet potatoes, broccoli, onions and summer squash. Candles were a fittingly obvious choice given the discovery of my ramshackle house of worship. They would provoke a comforting ominous elegancy to the old place. I was furthermore compelled to secure four pumpkins. Likewise, these were also a gift for the atmosphere. A shovel and a hardy rake for cleanup in and around the church. A local newspaper. Lots of water. Chapstick. I also managed to swipe an axe and a chair from a house I was lurking in for a bit before daybreak this morning. While these were not essential at the moment, I could not bring myself to resist taking them. Random souvenirs that cost me nothing and allow me to chop wood and sit.

Earlier this morning, before getting the groceries, I had awoken before the birds and finished off my last bit of bread and apple. Journeying into town, with enough darkness outside to remain unseen, I crept into a humble but fine house in the suburbs where a handsome couple lived with their young daughter. It is always so intoxicating to move around a person's home undetected while they slept. The hazard of almost getting caught numbs you very quickly then you slowly accept the weight of what you are doing in its fullness, but still choose to continue on through the rooms. The apprehension and uncertainty will just about dissolve completely during the very moment you see the unsuspecting duo sleeping soundly. When you realize that there may be others in the house your cerebrum begins to burn brilliantly with anticipation which encourages your cerebellum to take control and guide you to the child's room. This has now become a sort of mobile meditation. Something to lose yourself in but can still be in the moment enough to appreciate its greatness. Slinking terrifically to the room where the daughter sleeps, you approach the door. It vocalizes the faintest squeaks as it lazily allows you a better and better view of the sleeping child.

What now? Something you may ask yourself a dozen or more times on a spontaneous operation such as this. So you decide to probe the garage after delicately closing the bedroom door where the innocent young one continues to slumber. You grab a comfortable wicker chair with a cushion fixed to it and an insidious-looking felling axe. Do you leave the family inside dormant and secure or do you go back in for an alternative round of amusement? Best to leave now and progress on the betterment of your church Eden and be out of this home about the time that the daylight is sharp enough to expose your unsavory truck. If this kind of behavior was commonly accepted, or rather, not so quickly regarded as abominable, I would be recommending it to everyone.

Since there was still plenty of the day left I made use of the shovel and rake by removing the branches and leaves from the ground inside. A broom would have come in handy for the rest of the dirt still left on the floor but, I must say, the church is already looking more respectable. No point in moving the leftover dustings outside while there are still so many gaps in the wood that I could simply push it all into. I make a mental note to pick up a broom and enough scrap wood to cover these unwanted openings. By the time all the debris that I could manage to scoop up was moved outside and away from the building, and all of the branches were broken up into piles, it was beginning to get dark. It is always so satisfying to end a day having accomplished something, anything really. I cannot tell you how long it took me in life to realize this. Days upon days in a row when I was younger were spent doing absolutely nothing. I do mean nothing at all. Wake up. Sit inside. Wait. Go to sleep. Wake up, duplicate the previous day. I am now not able to get through one of those sorts of days without a tremendous amount of dejection afterwards. Now, here I am, making use of a day and ending it gratified.

The candles were set around the interior of the newly cleaned, but not exactly clean, structure. I still have approximately an hour of dim evening twilight left before these woods become fully darkened. My candles were lit. I brought the wicker chair up on the stage and sat down a few paces from the preacher's podium, looking out at my would-be disciples. A solemn copper haze from all the candles lit up the room just barely enough for me to see every part of it. It was mine now. My haven. My home. My Church of Elsewhere.

I made up my mind that it would not be worth it for me to pursue trying to buy this land. What would be the point? Surely, no one would have any reason to come all the way out here and kick me out for squatting. I seriously doubt anyone even knows this place exists in the first place. So, one of my options is to go to an irksome government building and find out who, if anyone, owns the land and try to purchase it. Which will of course be an extensive ordeal and likely have at least a few sets of eyes brought to this place, making the existence of it known to people besides myself. And that is only if I was able to purchase it. If not, then I become a legitimate trespasser from that day forward should I decide to keep harboring here. The other option is not telling a soul and go about my business undisturbed. Cognizant that even though I do not legally own this spot I know I can unofficially make it mine without any trouble or awareness from outsiders.

Easing further into my wicker throne and surrounded by a murky orange glow within my holy chamber I begin examining a pumpkin slightly bigger than a basketball. Beautiful things these fat gourds are. The ribs that encircle and form the rind mesmerize my hands while I roll it around between my palms. The feel of the waxy smooth skin stirs up all kinds of echoing childhood memories in pumpkin patches and autumn mischief. I hold it against my cheek to bear the sensation of touch on a new patch of flesh. When I finally collect the will to withdraw this embrace I immediately find myself plunging a knife into the body of my current infatuation. Incising and sawing commences without a thought. I now have a hole in the side where I can fit my hand. A hand goes in and a fist full of pulpy seeded guts comes out. This gets lobbed across the stage through a collapsed opening in the wall where a window was most likely situated. Hacking away at the side opposite the hole a face begins to develop. Two slightly lopsided triangular eyes and one sharp-toothed mouth with a grin that hooks up on each end nearly passing above the eyes on either side.

I place this on the podium and center my chair to face it. What kind of magnetism has carving this pumpkin bewitched me with? I cannot break eye contact with the newborn jack-o'-lantern. Is it still called a jack-o'-lantern without the lantern component? I am overcome with emotions that I find difficult to identify but would certainly be considered disturbing by normal folk. I am also aware that the pumpkin is not alive and will never communicate with me. But the fact that it is lifeless only seems to encourage my want to interact with it. Entertain it. Sure, I am isolated and presumably lonely. Though this is by personal preference to not be around others most of the time, save for a decent conversation once in a while or the useless urge I rarely ever get since leaving college to impress the fairer sex. Is that enough to insight this affinity to a pumpkin? While these thoughts and attempts of understanding myself pass through my mind's eye my physical eyes hold an increasingly all-consuming stare with the triangular ones; this seems to narrow everything else around me out of focus. Many moments pass before our gazes towards each other are severed due to the chill of cool air that gave me a sudden shiver. I cannot recall what was going through my head these last few moments. Am I simply coming unhinged?

It is clear that I should eat a few cold tortillas then retire for the night.

4

The water boils and gets poured into the little glass French press that I have already measured three heaping spoonfuls of ground coffee into. I give a quick stir and let it sit a few minutes before plunging. In this time, I pick up the newspaper acquired from the supply run yesterday.

Landing on the neighborhood news section there is instantly a recognizable face on the leading story. A missing woman named Avery Fletcher. Last seen leaving work from the office at the end of her shift a few days back. I know this office. No clues as to what may have happened. No history of mental illness, running away, incidents with others or anything of the sort. Husband was away on business and not considered a suspect. Neighbors exchanged waves with her as she left for work. The pizzaiolo, who sold her the slice at the pizza joint that she walks to on her lunch break nearly every day, says there was nothing out of the ordinary. I know this pizza joint. I know a lot of things that I prefer not to consider right now. And I suspect she will not be easy to locate.

There is one thing that distresses me about this article. It is how annoyed I am that they used the word 'pizzaiolo'.

I diced up some sweet potatoes and cooked them alongside the other vegetables for breakfast with a few handfuls of cereal while my camping stove took its time frying. I have not lost sight of the overwhelming musings I experienced last night after carving the pumpkin. Reeling from the notion of going back into my Elsewhere Church in a moment, to really get to work planning out how to fix it up, I am hit with even more delight remembering that I have three more pumpkins.

Today's full morning daylight helps me notice a truly wonderful sight. The character of the church is really starting to develop. Dark wooded walls as the backdrop for the slightly askew pews and staggered about candles. A pumpkin straight ahead down the aisle is commanding the stage from the podium perch. The place has really opened up since there are no longer desultory remnants of the forest occupying its floor. Without much else I can do at the moment I park myself down on the wicker throne that I reposition to be directly under a morning sunbeam coming through an orifice in the roof. With the orange preacher now adjusted to face me and his three kith by my side it becomes obvious that he is about to receive company just as soon as a visage is knifed into each of them.

The first of these remaining three gets oval eyes of very slightly different proportions. A triangle nose with the point aimed downward and mouth that goes straight across the face. This mouth is a simple, but not skillfully even, horizontal line right across with a handful of vertical slits going through it. Impossible to make out if he wears a smile or a frown, but can be interpreted either way and still be correct. When I finish carving this one I immediately start calling it Zipper, due to the zipper-like similarity of the mouth.

Next up is the largest, though not by much, and most oblong of the four pumpkins. It stands a bit taller as it is vertically longer, resembling an extreme case of birth molding in the head of a newborn baby that has been pulled from an overly pressurized womb. The knife sticks itself through the skin and works around at the flesh with my hand to guide it. This whole process has now become second nature and a blur as it happens. I snap back into consciousness and am left with a face full of features, at least more than the other two. She has eyes of an almost crescent shape or an elongated letter 'U', resembling two smiles. Two straight and inwardly slanted eyebrows form a corrupt leer that is only enhanced by the barbed and wavy half smile settled to the right of her mug. An upside down heart for a nose with half a dozen freckles poked in on each side. With no real lucid reasoning, I called her Blue.

The final one is affectionately named Ghost. This one is very uncomplicated. Eyes are a slanted oval style while the mouth is a long vertical oval shape. He is finished with a small equilateral triangle for a nose.

The guts and seeds sit in an unconfined pile next to me. Unlike the one carved last night, I remembered to separate and save these seeds when I was finished. When I stepped out to relieve myself I noticed a raven digging around in the discarded innards of last night's gourd and felt oddly nostalgic upon the sight. I boil today's kernels in salted water for a few minutes on my camp stove. This is meant to eliminate the chewy quality they present at the end of the drying process. It is now after noon and the sun is about as hot as it will get. I spread the seeds out on an old metal tray I retrieved from the truck and lay it in a well sunned spot by the church, moderately salted. My hope is that they will be palatable by tomorrow afternoon.

After a quick visit to my truck and a short walk back to the podium where my firstcarved is settled, I proceed to place two mason jars into his head. Formalin, a clear liquid preserving agent used on biological material, fills these jars. You will often see this in science labs with all kinds of different bodily parts, formerly belonging to living beings, submerged inside. The pint jars that I planted within the pumpkin's head that hold this substance also contain a magnificent green eye in each. I am remembering how surprisingly easy it was to take copious amounts of this fluid from the biology department a few weeks back at the university. With the true green peepers nestled in their new cavity, giving personality to the figure that holds it, a name finally comes to mind for the unnamed face. Avery.

Zipper, Blue and Ghost sit and watch me from a front pew while I eat a can of tuna fish on my woven cushioned seat upon the stage. Avery watches them while I try to consider how to make the most of my time for the next few days, but I ultimately end up zoning out for a bit.

Thoughts of malevolence eventually slip into my daydreaming. The realization that I only scarcely act on my grisly impulses compared to how often I have them begins to ignite a sense of defeat within me. Urges must be satisfied in all beings at some point, even if only to a minor degree. I guess I am securing a minor degree of satisfaction on occasion, but the toll that accumulates within me for what my spirit considers sufficient is going to keep piling up and eventually erupt. This land with this church was all I ever wanted for myself. Now that I have it I want more. Something divinely fulfilling rather than physically. I wonder if anyone is ever eternally gratified with life after they acquire or achieve the thing they think they want most. Can this notion of being truly content actually just be a revolving door of wants and expectations that are ever-changing every time the spinning makes a complete rotation?

I now look out into the solid gazes of my creations on the pews. There is a sense of expectation towards me coming from them. The sun fades and an airy blue hue sets upon the room. I get up and light the candles before returning to my chair. This does not break the tensity of my senses. Perhaps we need to accept that there is no permanent quenching of thirst. That it is just a constant back and forth between the two, thirst and quench. And if we realize this then we can create a journey for ourselves based on that criteria and be conscious to the fact that what we are doing to flood the drought is temporary. To never try and make our missions feel complete, but to make them more frequent. Keep the door spinning, and quickly. Keep the thirst coming back in order to quench it sooner. Dry everything in order to be able to open the flood gates. Complete indulgence is a key part of the solution.

-5-

Last night was one of the greatest nights of sleep I have had in a long time. It felt almost as if I had been drugged with something that blissfully induces comfort and rest. With an essence of enlivened optimism and excitement but without the anxiousness that goes along with it. I feel a purposeful momentum building inside me. With this newfound force I jump in my truck and head out for a drive after bidding the pumpkins a quick goodbye.

Going west into upstate New York was an easy choice as I have always heard about the expansive woods, gorges, rivers and all around secluded wildernesses here from a handful of peers at college. Most people have an immediate impression that all of New York is like New York City, according to these peers. The second you say you are from New York people get the idea of the bustling metropolis instead of what most of the state actually is, they would explain to me. This is what I have come here to experience. I have no idea how far or how long I have actually driven but I can be certain that I am closer to Canada than to the Elsewhere Church.

As luck would have it a pumpkin patch is nearing. A decision is made that the four back home could use some

32

company. The old farm is tucked far away from anything. I imagine there are many of these farms around this area and that they are relatively unfrequented. The character of the sign for this farm was a good indication of this assumption. It looked like a piece of wood ripped from an ancient barn and was shabbily placed on that lonesome backroad. An aged man in overalls approaches me and informs me I am free to roam. It seems this is primarily a vineyard. I walk through countless rows of grape vines supported by wire trellises before I almost begin to deem myself lost. My wandering does eventually take me to a small but full pumpkin patch. The old farmer has cleverly created an advantage for his clientele by placing wheelbarrows by the patch. I load up a few large white pumpkins and a few smallish blue ones. I can see an incredibly more manageable path back to the truck now that I have my bearings. The elderly fellow is there to greet me and take my money with the accompaniment of his wife. I then carry on to roam about on the backroads in my truck. The bare wilds of this whole region is inspiring and unexpected to me as someone who has never been here, as my student peers have sharply guessed. The occasional townships I pass are drastically uninhabited, save for a few families. This is not to give the impression that there is any kind of bleakness to their existence. It is actually quite enviable. They are thriving in their small Dutch colonial homes and lands. Paralleling the long forgotten times of New England settlement. I come upon a sign that reads:

Entering Bok
Unincorporated
Settled In 1791

Following a densely forested road, with tree branches that reach out overhead nearly forming a tunnel for me to move through, I come upon a young woman walking alone. With my curiosity about Bok getting the better of me it seems right to consider stopping to ask her all the burning questions in my head. I estimate her to be in her mid-twenties, possibly early twenties. As I draw nearer to her I can see she is wearing an old fashioned dark blue and white dress with a full skirt and long sleeves. It is noticeably fitting for the atmosphere. Similar to what the colonist women wore or even what the Amish ones display today. I thought my approach and introduction would have startled her but she was totally unfazed.

"Hello," I said, not sure if I should say more in case the girl was not interested in interacting.

She stops and fully faces me while I, in turn, bring the truck to a stop from a slow crawl and shift into park.

She proceeds to say, "Hello," in a calm and welcoming tone.

I feel as though her and her people must be extremely trusting out here as they probably have never had to deal with much trouble from others. This trusting nature makes me wonder why absence of conflict might equal trust. Paranoia could have festered over time and caused someone like this to be overly cautious from lack of experience in dealing with hostile confrontation. I am swimming with inquiries about the village but before I could settle on which to ask first I found myself feverishly hopping to the passenger side of the truck bench and reaching through the open window to grab her light brown hair. With a few swift tugs towards me her head collides into the blue-grey door and she is knocked unconscious.

"About time. Welcome," I say softly to the girl as she flutters her eyes open on the front pew to the left.

On the opposite side of the aisle, where my three round congregants sit, she begins to try raising up from her slumped over position. This takes her a moment. Not only because of the blunt trauma to her head, but also due to the black electrical tape wrapped around her wrists and ankles. I give her time to gather herself and glance around before we begin. Dry blood cakes up patches of hair above her chestnut brown eyes. I find it a good idea to ruffle a wet towel around her face and bloody locks to clean the girl up some.

"That town you come from, Bok, it really is something. I always wished I could have been raised in a village like that. One hidden in nature and not drawn into every evolution that time had to impose on the world."

"Where have you taken me? Wh-where are we?"

"Well, not in Bok. Not even close. We are elsewhere. A church, as you can see."

The sun is setting and darkness is beginning to choke out the light. I break our focus on each other to ignite the candles. The church is lit up once again in that brilliant orange haze that consistently proves to be a worthy visual counterpart to the dimming blue evening surrounding us outside.

"Please let me go. How long was I out for? I'm sore all over."

"I can't. And a long time, hours. I made sure of that. The soreness makes sense. Let me start from where you finished."

I go on to tell her, in as much detail as I can, everything that happened after bashing her head into my truck's door and leading right up to where we are at this moment. I let go of her head after its last impact to my passenger door. She dropped crudely to the ground and I quickly got out and dragged her conveniently lightweight but troublesome limp body to the back of my truck and loaded her up. I had arrived in Bok just minutes prior to this and I could not help but investigate the village. Old farmsteads set on little personal vineyards. Individual, single family sized corn, potato and hay plots. With all kinds of humble orchards comprised of only a few different fruit-bearing trees per each home. On most of the properties chickens could be seen free ranging confidently around the gardens. An occasional cow or pig or goat would be moseying around a pen of their own. People sat on porches or were in the field using dated tools.

As I am explaining these things that she already knows about her own community a dry cough breaks out from her throat. I quickly bring a coffee mug filled with water I had prepared to offer her a while back when she was passed out, but had forgotten about. When I start to bring it closer to her face she pulls back slightly while looking me directly in the eyes; one eyebrow cocked up with an air of distrust. So I bring the mug to my own lips and take a tiny sip to show her it is not poison.

"You should really just drink this," I tell her in a faintly demanding way, implying both that it is good for her to get some fluids and also that she does not have much of a choice anyway.

After she allowed me to pour half the mug of water into her mouth and gulped it down, her voice piped out.

"Let me go. Now!"

This was a noticeably desperate attempt to conquer me while realizing how hopeless her situation was. There was definitely a stronger sense of panic brewing inside her that she could not hide. My reaction to this command was to grab her shoulders firmly and push her back, hard against the pew. This causes her to hunch over with utter startlement as tears begin to well up. I again strongly grip a shoulder and carelessly pull her upright, making sure she feels the strength I am willing to use. There is now a tense silence between us that needs to be broken.

I ask, "So what's the deal with your old fashioned way of life? Are you in some sort of cult or an Amish-like belief system? It's hard to believe there are still societies in this country that use hand plows to till their farms or wear outdated clothes, like the dress you have on now, that aren't part of some eccentric religion."

She chokes back her despair and answers bravely, "Not a cult or a religion, as far as I see it. We just appreciate working hard each day to feed ourselves. Our elders taught us that a slothful lifestyle will lead to mental unrest. And we wear all kinds of different clothes. We are aware this isn't considered normal, but I like it. There's many communities like ours scattered around the area, you could see for yourself."

"I intend to."

The way she just spoke to me just now was with a mellow confidence. Maybe because she found comfort in talking about her home. I also felt this from her when she was on the roadside talking to me. At first it seemed like naive trust. The more she shows this fleeting confident side to me it feels as if it was not a pure trusting nature at all in the beginning but more like she did not care what happened to her, so there was no need to have her defenses up. It is also entirely possible that I am reading into this wrong. My head is all over the place to begin with from all of the excitement. There is definitely a level of intelligence present in this one which makes her presence somewhat difficult to read.

I go on explaining what happened. I tell her how as I was driving through Bok, with her unconscious self in my truck bed, I imagined which of the farmhouses she might belong to. An exercise to keep the road trip amusing. It could have been any of them. When it started to drag I turned to head back towards home.

"I wish I had woken up and screamed or jumped from the truck! My neighbors would have beaten you to a pulp and you would be locked away in our barn right now!" she interjected with sharp eyes fixed on me.

I thought about wringing her neck at this hypothetical threat, but instead I told her how there was not the slightest bit of worry in my mind about her waking up.

"Did I forget to mention I had you hooked up to an ether inhaler?"

Another item to add to the list of spoils I carried off from Ole Miss University. A relic from anesthesiological history dating back to the mid-eighteen hundreds that was stowed away in the vaults of the medical department. It is an airtight quart-sized glass jar with a hose attached to the top. On the other end of this hose is a rubber apparatus that covers a person's nose and fastens around the head. Inside the jar houses a few sponges soaked in ether, two more acquired items courtesy of the Mississippi University. The fumes have only one place to go; through the tube and into her, ensuring she stayed knocked out until we got here. Just for good measure and to make sure that no prying eyes caught sight of my secret parcel, I was keen to stop back at the remote pumpkin patch to load up more pumpkins. I piled enough around and a few on top of the girl to keep her hidden. The rest of the drive back was mostly uneventful apart from the coyote I ran over. The beast could not make up its mind about whether or not it wanted to be in my direct path or just out of it. At the last moment it made a decision that cost its life.

While I consider this coyote, a wavy feeling overcomes me. I decide to follow this train of thought for a moment.

I think we unawarely come into these two options, like the coyote had, of quickly deciding life or death often but our human brains are just quicker in terms of determining our survival than this canine, for example. Now I am certain that the little sip I took of the girl's water had enough acid in it to get me high. I am relieved that this is familiar territory for me or I might start to fluster.

"Anyway," I say, snapping out of this philosophizing, "we arrived at my church and you were hauled to where you're sitting now. Then I bound you with electrical tape."

A quick wrap up to the story of the day then brought my eyes from their comfortable fixation on the floor, which was starting to come alive with breathing ripples, to the girl on the bench. Her own stare towards the floor was visibly not reflecting the same sense of comfort as I felt. More like dread. Much more than she was feeling moments ago, I presume.

-7-

It is confirmed. The LSD I found hidden in the floor of this old church is still impressively potent. The girl spent the last little while, since I told her about the drugs she was unknowingly given, zoning out in trippy terror. She is not familiar with this sort of thing at all. Surely being abducted and bound in a decaying church is something quite unfamiliar to her as well. She slumps herself over in that familiar position she has been in a few times already. Though, this time she almost looks at ease about it.

She gazes upwards like a catatonic cat waiting to be operated on. I crouch down to see what she is so interested in. Her line of vision goes right through the gap in the roof to a tree branch lightly dancing just beyond. When I see this I take a seat on the floor in front of her and stare at the same tree limb. I watch all the leaves of this branch start to breathe in beautiful rhythm. The tips wrap around themselves and back out again while morphing color and mood. For a second I feel like they are breathing for me and have to remind myself to take breaths. Just five tabs of the acid chopped up small and dropped into a cup of water and one puny sip of it did this to me. As someone who has taken high doses of this substance, on multiple occasions, I can understand what this girl might be feeling and I am sure it is way too intense for her to handle as a first and only-timer. Keeping control will not be easy.

I look over at her and she is still staring out. Now with tears effortlessly pouring out of her ducts and streaming sideways down her resting face.

"What's your name?" I ask coarsely with no desire to alleviate her distress by using a comforting tone.

She speedily responds, barely moving her lips as if she were talking in her sleep, "Eeka."

"Well, Eeka," I turn toward her and lift myself off the ground, "I'm going to cut the tape off your hands."

If she were in her right mind I would have seen a flicker
of hope in those brown eyes. Since she was so deep into the acid
trip I don't think hope even crossed her mind. Hope and
hopeless no longer existed in her world. Her hands are free now
and she has not moved at all. They are still pressing against her
chest like they would in a fetal position.

My legs are wobbly now that I am standing, but I
manage to walk over to the stage and pull the wicker chair down
to set it in front of Eeka. While she was unconscious earlier I
managed to unload some of the new pumpkins into Elsewhere
with us. I take one of the big white ones into my lap and cut a
circle around the stem. It gets removed then the guts and seeds
follow. Eeka's wonder is now on me. As I take my time carving
a face into the pumpkin my only thoughts are with Eeka and
what she might be seeing through her eyes. The melting of
orange haziness surrounding us, blurring into the white
pumpkin she is fixated on; all filtered through the foggy lens of
LSD induced delirium. I was not especially creative with this
face. Standard triangle eyes. Triangle nose. Smiling and with a
few squared teeth thrown in. My arms are wobbly now from all
the muscle put into carving. I flip this white gourd over so the
bottom is now on top and proceed to cut a large hole in it. When
the cutting is done I stand full and tall and place it over my
head. Her eyes widen and she pulls herself up in a sitting
position for the first time since she laid down. The brown iris in
each is totally black. Dilated to the highest degree and
completely focused on me and my heavy gourd veil. I am not
able to tell if she still feels dread from the expression on her
face, but there is an overwhelming facade of awe.

"I like what you had to say earlier, about your elders
discouraging you from slothful living. Maybe it's the drugs
talking but it has really resonated with me. This feels like a gift

you have given me that I can integrate into my life, moving forward," I say with muffled words from the pumpkin over my face and a touch of vulnerability, in that I was allowing myself to open up like this.

I am typically fine with embracing my stubbornness towards not letting other people affect me.

"I don't believe a word you say. You kidnapped me, drugged me twice now and I've lost count how many times you've struck me. You want to make an improvement on your way of living? Well… I. Don't. Care! Why would I care about anything you are saying? You are an awful person and it should be obvious how to fix yourself. I mean, look around you," she says, giving me some understanding of where her current point of view is.

"Don't believe me, you say?"

I walk over to the podium and reach up to get Avery. A slow walk over to Eeka and a solemn approach in my walking jack-o'-lantern form gives her a moment to readjust her nerves. I stand in front of her with Avery to my torso, at eye level with the girl at the peak of an acid trip. She is looking up at my carved white, nearly toothless grinning face.

I gravely tell her, "Look into my eyes. Do you see how serious I am?"

She already knows I mean Avery's eyes, not my own. So she obeys and shifts her focus to the two tilted triangular holes in front of her. It understandably takes her a few seconds to adjust her vision from the melting perception she is experiencing to a consolidated sight. Terror sweeps across her face when she finally realizes what it is she is seeing. Two human eyes. Severed from their owner and floating lifelessly in jars. Her eyes flutter but remain totally anchored to the horror before her.

"Nobody comes to the Elsewhere Church and doesn't get stuck with my knife."

I gently set Avery down on the edge of the stage and turn back to face Eeka.

"Just ask those guys," I say while pointing the knife to the three carved faces sitting on the other pew.

Eeka runs her open hands up and down her face and hair and giggles maniacally. During one of these motions I charge towards her and plunge my knife downward through the top of her head. Her hands drop from her face and the only thing keeping her lifeless body propped up now is me holding the knife.

-8-

Eeka was buried a few miles from the church. I dragged her and a shovel out the next morning in a big tarp. No eulogy or moment of silence; she didn't matter to me. I owe her nothing. Her zombified eyes stood fixed in a state of looking up and began to pale while a permanent crooked slack-jaw stole focus of her face in a most unpleasant way. The thick knife hole in the top of her skull where I speared her was darkening as the wound and blood had oxidized since its liberation from the confines of her body. I illuminated her pineal gland with the acid and then extinguished that third eye with a blade. The grave took over two hours to dig a proper depth and I resent Eeka for this. I rolled her into the pit after delivering a few fierce kicks to the stomach and then sealed her up with fresh earth.

Exhaustion is beginning to take hold. The road trip through upstate New York yesterday would normally be enough to drain me. When you add an adequate drug trip followed by little sleep and a morning of hiking, hauling and digging all with the complete absence of nourishment, it would sufficiently enervate anyone. While I am physically depleted, a spark of motivation burns in my psyche. I soon find myself driving down the mountain and back into Saint Ox. It is a particularly warm day today, compared to the last few. I get a better layout of the town while aimlessly driving around. I pass a grocery store, different from the one I shopped at the other day, the post office, gas stations, people walking the sidewalk with their children and sweethearts. A big park containing an ample amount of playground structures for the kids and exercise apparatuses for those looking to publicly shape themselves.

An old traditional American diner called The Buzzy Bee Diner catches my attention and spawns significant hunger, which at this point could be considered starvation. The only sustenance I have had in the last day was a handful of pumpkin seeds. With this realization I end up inside The Buzzy Bee Diner. The hostess is welcoming and I opt for a seat at the counter, near to where they cook the food rather than have her walk me to a booth or table. A retro diner vibe is made clear with the furniture in their nineteen-fifties fashion. For how faded the sky blue and cherry red vinyl on the booths were, I would believe it if these are actually from the fifties and not recreations. Framed ads for cigarettes and kitchen wares from days long gone hung all over the walls. In the booths there were nickel-fed miniature jukeboxes. On the kitchen bar where I seated myself there sat one of those little machines that enigmatically answers the questions you ask. A devilish imp's head rests atop this square, cardinal red, tin device. All my burning questions could be resolved for just a dime. I go ahead and order a stack of pancakes and carrot juice from the large oily man working the griddle in front of me.

In turn he yells out, "One Jayne Mansfield and a glass of orange root."

He gave me a vexed look as he said that last part. I understand that this was probably because not many customers ever order carrot juice. Either way, I wanted to gut him for that look. The woman at the other end of the counter writes down the order and she heads in the back to make the juice while the stout cook gets to work on the food.

It now dawns on me who Jayne Mansfield is. This tapped into a very distant memory of mine.

My neighbors growing up were fans and had pictures of her on the walls of their house. We watched her movies more than I care to remember and I would always be told a story or two about her when we were over these neighbor's house for dinner. Jayne Mansfield was an actress in the fifties and sixties with some additional work modeling nude for reputable magazines and calendars. She was an industry peer of Marylin Monroe, though never becoming as much of a household name as Marylin. This is a fact that greatly bothers me more and more as I sit here thinking about it. Jayne was much more talented and all around more attractive than Marylin Monroe. Maybe I feel this way due to the exposure I had to her at a young age, a sort of imprinting. But from an attempted standpoint of neutrality, I still feel Jayne was all around more worthy. Not to mention Jayne Mansfield was significantly more professional and there was no existence of a barbiturate addiction.

I am thankful that there is no one near me or even paying attention to me because I fear that my sense of unrest is highly observable at the moment. The carrot juice is brought to me just after I collect myself from this incidental frustration.

I recall a big part of the discussion at the neighbors house was Jaynes death. She was a passenger in a car along with her attorney and three children. The Buick they were traveling in late that night collided into a much slower moving tractor-trailer truck, instantly killing her, the attorney, their driver and a few small dogs they had with them. The children, however, all made it out alive. These neighbors of mine once mentioned how they tracked down and purchased a photo of the car crash scene. After dinner all the adults passed it around with looks of intense unpleasantness and vocalized how it was such a shame for all sorts of reasons; so young, all that talent, those poor children, that beautiful car. Us children were forbidden to see this photo. Deemed inappropriate for our developing sensibilities.

One night, not too long after, I snuck into their house through a kitchen window while they slept. I had paid full attention to where they kept that photo so it was not hard to locate when I invaded their home. The little drawer inside the tall cabinet to the right of the fireplace. I sat down on the reclining chair for twenty minutes and examined the image. Even though it was black and white I could still make out every detail. The car was totaled. Jayne was still sitting there in the passenger seat but with bloody legs and a vaguely contorted upper half. She was facing the camera one last time. The very top of her head was not visible because it lay behind the mangled parts of the car's roof. Rumor has it that her skull cap had been severed and was somewhere else in the car entirely, but this is impossible to tell from the photo. When I put the photo back an urge overcame me. Tiptoeing down the hall I get to the door of the married couple that I lived next door to. I watched them sleep with all the images of the car wreck circling my mind for a while before going home and getting to sleep myself.

I now wonder what it felt like for Eeka when I executed her. When the knife hungrily went through her skull and fed into her brain. My stomach growls at the frenzied excitement I felt last night. Remembering this is invoking my appetite.

I bring these thoughts to that impish devil's head, that teeters on top of the tin box in front of me, with a shiny dime to hire his wisdom and quietly ask my question.

"Was she still alive when I shook her head back and forth from the handle of my knife?"

Animating her like that still gladdens me to no end.

I move the creatures plastic head to the side and the tin spits out a novelty card that reads:

THE ANSWER YOU SEEK IS ALREADY KNOWN.
MORE IMPORTANTLY, IT DOES NOT MATTER.

I am not sure why, but I approve of this answer. My pancakes are placed before me and I say a darkly cryptic, "Thank you."

This is meant for the wise beast I have just employed for knowledge but I allowed the breakfast chef to accept it instead. I left forgetting to ask why he calls the order a 'Jayne Mansfield' and wondering if this is a saying at diners everywhere.

9

Without much else to do in town besides fill up my water at a gas station, I plan to make way back out to my mountain forest refuge. I take this last opportunity in town to use the restroom. On the way out after relieving myself I notice the twenty-five cent dispensers containing an assortment of condoms, lube and erection pills. Among the pills is an older brand of the Spanish fly variety that piques my interest. There is a chemical in this Spanish fly that has been long banned in this country due to the toxicity level which is essentially a poison. A few decades ago there were companies in Mexico that manufactured this authentic Spanish fly and heaps of the stuff made it over the border before it was tested. They imported the shiny green male beetles from Asia and Europe to extract cantharidin, the poisonous chemical that the insects naturally create, and put small traces of it in the pill. While cantharidin has been proven and used as an aphrodisiac in many parts of the world throughout history, there is even more proof that to become harmfully poisoned from it takes a very insignificant amount. Hence, the reason it has been banned for ages.

I have the cashier break a five dollar bill for me so I can purchase every one of these Spanish fly packets, quarter by quarter. When the dispenser in the mens room is tapped out I offer to buy every single one in the back that they may have left. The cashier, who is presumably also the owner, obliges and twenty-eight dollars later I leave the store with a box of arousal pills or a box of poison, depending on who you ask. At the pump is a younger couple talking about that missing Avery woman. I stay and wash my windows with the supplied blue liquid and squeegee in order to eavesdrop longer. From what I gather, the police suspect foul play. This seems like an obvious conclusion to me. A small lake near her house has been dredged with no results and a plan to dredge another one is underway. They will not find her this way.

As I zigzag my way through town in the direction of my home there comes a field I have not passed before. Stalls and open tents are set up in true small town flea market style. The cheeky sign at the grassy entrance says they are open every weekend and any day of the week that has nice enough weather. I pull in and poke around. Nothing interests me too much. There are a lot of locally made food items like honey, jams and syrups; key items to a true New England market. I left with an antique book about the history of Saint Ox. It cost me nothing since I slipped it under my shirt while passing the booth of a wrinkly half-asleep elderly man. Halfway to my truck I can see the ridiculously pricey tag wedged and sticking out of the pages.

-10-

My poor gourd children are beginning to soften. Their faces begin to sag, much like everyone's will someday in a long enough timeframe. If there were a way to preserve them more than a week before the rot starts to take over I would be in high spirits. I believe I feel more for these jack-o'lanterns in the short time I have known them than I ever have for another human being. I will have to search my memory to make sure this is true, but I do not ever remember having these kinds of roughly emotional attachments to anybody. To watch these pumpkin beings wither and die in front of me strikes a nerve I did not know I had. My only choice is to carve new ones in the same fashion and continue this cycle of rebirth for my companions.

For now, I am drained of energy. Just about all that I can do is relax. I pull my padding and sleeping bag out from the truck and lay it all down on the stage in the Elsewhere Church. It has not quite started to get dark yet but I light all the candles anyway in anticipation. This is one of those times when you do not realize how tired your body is until you actually lay down. The muscles everywhere on my body ache with unrest but are slowly acclimating to a comfortable state. Reading the book I swiped is my only mission for the rest of today.

A Meticulous History Of Saint Ox. Written forty-one years ago in nineteen fifty-six.

It details the two equally possible origins of the name Saint Ox. The first being that it came from a sect of French Catholic colonists. Named for Saint Luke who is often depicted as an ox in religious works of art and texts. It goes on to talk about how the ox represents sacrifices, which I find interesting enough to keep reading in my tired state. But, I see the second possibility as more interesting.

It claims that there were a small number of Greek colonists that came to the Spanish-ruled Florida colony in the mid-seventeen hundreds. While the ideas of the old Greek Mythological faiths were put to rest about eight-hundred years prior to their coming to the Florida region, it is still believed that there were many worshippers left in the world and some were among these settlers. Their god of choice was said to be Apollo, the sun god. For this reason they chose Florida, the sunshine state as it is now known today. They moved around different parts of Florida throughout the rest of the seventeen hundreds, ineffectively able to colonize anywhere and put down roots. Some stayed in Florida while many others splintered off and headed in different directions. One of these factions landed in northwestern Massachusetts and started up a little village. While in New England, they were still surrounded mostly by Catholics and Protestants and others of the sort. The old gods were outnumbered and would surely be run out if the Greeks were open about their ideology. So they set up their village and gave a clearly disguised name. Ox was meant to symbolize Apollo as he was also the god of cattle or oxen, which were a big part of their livelihood. They then added Saint to the name to appeal to the other colonists' holy sensibilities and further obscure their true religious labeling of the village.

This is the extent of my willpower for staying awake. I am happy to end this feverishly hectic day with some local folklore. The book goes next to my sleeping bag on the church's stage. The candles burn down while I sleep the entire night with no waking disturbances as the rotting pumpkins ceaselessly watch over me.

-11-

An explosion of bright sensations pries my awareness fully open, like a tightly closed oyster from an inert state. I am face down on a beach but gaining strength as I pull myself up. It is unusually light out for how grey the sky above is. Clouds and fog are overhead in every direction above but strangely radiant and glowing everywhere on my level. The heavens weep while I bask in a sandy Eden of confusion. Further from me, on this endless shore, seems to be a village just after the small dunes ahead. I am only now gathering enough stability in my legs to walk. My thoughts are staggered. I cannot keep myself focused on trying to figure out what exactly is going on; where I am, what to do, who I am. My vision is fragmented as well. What I am seeing, with every few careful steps, is a coastline. This shoreline view cuts away in sporadic moments and then I will suddenly be seeing rocks in front of me. My sight will cut back to this beach in another instant and then a quick few seconds of clouds are all around me. Not abruptly in a falling state, but just surrounded by clouds. I try to reason with myself when this happens.

Everything is fine, if you panic everything will not be fine, so just go with it.

This 'just go with it' voice of reason is helping, but it should not be. I am utterly confused on the inside but desperately keeping this mantra to trick and distract myself from the actual total uncertainty that is happening in every aspect of this experience. I arrive at the dunes bizarrely fast. I can sense myself here in the sand dunes that I have arrived at and also back behind myself one hundred paces, simultaneously.

Just go with it and do not consider why. Everything is as it should be.

Self-deception, but it keeps the hysteria at bay.

My legs waver onward past the dunes. The village I previously saw as a distant mirage becomes distinct. This village is not large by any means. There are maybe ten houses which makes it more of a neighborhood than a village. No buildings other than homes. But these homes are extremely unlivable. They are darkly colored, not from their paint but from their age or perhaps just all together ragged conditions. Faded wooden houses with tattered sheets to cover the glassless windows. Roofs with large gaps bitten out of them. Cracks in all parts of the structures, especially the walls, due to ever-shifting foundations. Loose beams and wood siding hanging from random spots all around. I assume these houses would be condemned if this is the sort of world where an agency exists to authorize such an action.

I am still in the openness of the beach and, before I can take the awkward initiative to move toward the dilapidated suburb again, I am met with a brushing hand down my right arm. I am too insensible to react the way I normally would, by being startled and defensive. No, I simply make a stupefied turn towards the unexpected phenomena.

I am in a heavily leafed tree. Now I am back on the beach.

Standing beside me is Eeka. Radiantly beautiful, a physical feature I do not notice in people much anymore but, for some reason, is indisputable to me in this moment. Her brown hair is lightly flowing towards the direction I came from.

She opens her mouth and her words drift out in slowish motion, "Have you gone?"

Her eyes motion towards the eerie set of homes on this perplexing beach. At first I could not make sense of the words she was saying. I replayed her lip movement in my mind a few times before I decided I understood.

Everything is as it should be. I am supposed to be confused, I think.

"I am going now," I reply, with my words coming out of me at the same lumbering pace as hers.

We are both walking side by side into the decaying hamlet. She is humming, in a hauntingly feminine tone, a melody that seems so fitting and natural. I almost feel that it is coming from inside of me, not from outside. I am looking at each building as we glide aimlessly around to the rhythm of her wistful tune. Her song stops and I immediately miss it dearly. In the short while since she started the tune I feel I have begun to depend on it.

We are in front of one of the run down homes. Eeka looks at me and I look back at her while she holds out a stretched arm and points to the front door. No words are necessary. She wants me to go in. Do not think, just go with it, I conclude.

In the blink of an eye I am already through the front door and standing alone in the foyer. A large rotting staircase sits in front of me that goes up to a hallway which extends left and right at the top. A balcony overlooks down onto where I am standing. Downstairs, both sides of me have entranceways into large living rooms that each lead to somewhere invisible from where I stand.

I am stuck in a rocky crevice; a tight slot canyon of some kind. Now I am back in the dank foyer of the house.

My eyes catch the chilling sight of three figures coming down the stairs in a line. Marching in matching steps. This unsettles my mind but my body does not tense up as if it were so. Ragged grey suits worn by all three. Drooping heads with their mouths agape and slanted. Wide open and misshapen dead-eyes. Step by step they ascend the stairs. Clearer now, I know who they are. Representations I could never mistake in this form or the forms I am used to them as. It was only moments ago I was watching them watch me fall asleep.

I am somehow surrounded by large pieces of unbroken stained glass. In a flash, I am once again in the foyer.

Zipper, Blue and Ghost stand before me with lamented appearances, each harrowingly equivalent but dissimilar to the look I carved for them days ago. Blue, in the middle, steps forward. Her eyes that were once smiles have flattened down due to her previously ovaloid head now being a deflated squash of its former self. The sagging barbed wire shaped mouth begins to move with weighted effort.

She says, "You let us molder and spoil without any attempt at preserving," low-voiced and slowly.

I am almost in complete disbelief but manage to say, "How can I possibly preserve a gutted pumpkin longer than this?"

"Idle undertaker!" scorns Ghost. "You have toyed with the idea of rebirth for us already. Put our corpses aside and create again."

I become sorrowful as their lifeless and almost wrathful black eyes stare me down. Waves begin to crash outside where it was once calm. The world around me darkens further and rain starts to fall, hitting us by way of all the missing sections in the roof. Eeka emerges next to me once more and I look over at her for a moment. Her head is bowed in a solemn nod. When my attention moves back in front of me the three suited pumpkin golems are gone. No, they are crouched way down low on all fours in a most disturbing manner. The rain cascades down heavier and much colder. Between the unusual sight I am witnessing and this freezing rain showering me I begin an uneasy series of quivers. The motionless humanoid pumpkins now look up at me all at once. I am taken back from this unnerving act. They then lurch up on hind legs and dash rapidly in different directions, still semi-squatted on all fours, like three of the fastest spiders I have ever seen. One of them goes through the room to the left, the other to the right and the last up the stairs. It was an unexpectedly horrific sight. The rain falls heavy as ever and becomes increasingly colder every second. I take one step backwards and...

I jolt up in my sleeping bag to a sitting position. Tears are running down my face with frigid air biting every piece of skin that is not covered. My heart races and my body shivers. I can just barely see my breath while I huff and puff. The candles still flicker dimly but with plenty of life left in them.

I have not been able to shake this weeping that has me hexed. As I look around, attempting to recover, the audience that has been watching me comes to my field of vision. They look even more rotted than I remember and their dreary lifeless gazes are equivalent to those in my dream. Avery still sits upon the podium, decaying but with a spark of life in his eyes. The glow from the candles onto the glass jars of eyes inside him are the cause for his remaining spirit. My sobs have still not let up. I begin to wonder why Avery, with his transplanted eyes that would have fit justly into this dream, was not there. Even Eeka was represented, though not in pumpkin form. My attention is turned towards her jack-o'lantern, or rather, the one I shaped just before masking myself with it and mortally impaling her head. Eeka had come back from the dead to haunt my dreams. A revenant in her own right. I am chilled to the bone and irritated more at the fact that I am still sobbing with unidentified emotion that this dream has brought on. I am trying to recall how the song Eeka was humming went, but it is no use. It is about as hard to do as making sense of the quick back and forth location changes that happens in dreams or even as hard as interpreting the dream itself.

After a quick yell to break the crying spell, I reach into the pillow for my journal and write this dream down before it slips away.

-12-

It has warmed up over the past few days, but is obvious that I should prepare for the cold weather to come. Moving into mid-October it seems I have gotten away with the near extent of warmer temperatures that mother nature is willing to give up here in the mountains. Without giving much more thought to this I go ahead and pick up a few more orange pumpkins from town to satisfy the requisition of my three dream spirits. I could have made it easy on myself and used the white pumpkins or even the small blue ones I picked up from the farm in New York, but think it is best to play it safe and aim for as faithful re-creations as possible. The grocery store has plenty of fresh ones in stock which thankfully tells me that the growing season has not ended yet. I grab three of them that seem to be the proper size along with a loaf of French bread, produce, water, toilet tissue, and canned goods. While checking out I think it might be time to figure out a way to make more money in the near future. I am not in any major rush for this on account of the decent size of my savings, especially now that I do not plan on using it to pay for land. But my funds are dwindling and buying pumpkins this consistently is not helping.

Before making my way back up to the Church of Elsewhere I stop at the Saint Ox Pool And Recreation Center to have a free shower in the locker room. The water pours over me and I see a rusty reddish color pooling up by the drain. It must be Eeka's blood that dried itself on spots of my skin that remain a mystery. Something about showering always sparks introspection. It could be the extreme state of comfortable vulnerability from being completely naked and wet in a tiny room. This, for me, breaks down mental defenses from deep thought and triggers the soul to stir the mind. Match that with the sight of the day-old blood from a young woman washing off me and I have a good reason for psychic reflection.

These thoughts of mine soar to her hometown of Bok. I cannot let go of wondering about their lifestyle. Perhaps I should have kept Eeka around a bit longer to have her detail the village more. It is hard to understand why I am so drawn to a place like this. This small community living seems like it would be incredibly irritating and way too personal for me to handle without quickly giving in to my grisly impulses. Maybe, deep down, I yearn for a sense of community for myself. Could this be what I am trying to develop with my pumpkins? Is the inanimateness of my carved company the key to the tolerative nature I maintain in their presence? This train of thought stays with me after I leave the shower building. I keep wondering if it would ever truly be possible for me to be around others for a long run. Even at college I did not get to test this as I lived in an apartment off campus and mostly kept to myself. The few friendships I did have were kept mild and distanced. Hardly anything most would even label as friends.

I have just exited the town and am passing a few farms before the road ascends into my wilderness. One of these farms has a fence-line close to the road with handfuls of chickens roaming around. They are all in groups except for one. A younger looking pullet that is mostly a dark orange, almost light brown, color with black spots and streaks throughout the feathering. I decide to put my pondering to the test and see if I could endure living with another live being for a while. Best to start small with assessments like this.

The truck is parked and I climb the fence. The chickens in their groups scurry away as expected. What is unexpected was the lonesome orange with black one that comes trotting towards me. I surely thought that in order to catch any of these hens I would have to corner them and use force. This one essentially leapt into my arms when I squatted down to beckon her closer. I take a quick look around to make sure no one is watching and when I am sure the coast is clear of any spies I hop back over the fence. With hen in hand we get in the car. Her in the passenger seat. And I, in the drivers', making haste to Elsewhere.

The chicken made herself at home in the church. I had parked the truck right up next to the building and when I opened my door and got out she was following immediately behind me with a few hops across the seats and a light flap to ease her landing on the ground. I already decided that I would not try to train or control her. If she went to flee it was not my purpose to retrieve and contain the beast. Regardless of my unwillingness to govern her, she behaved like a properly governed chicken anyway. The pullet shadows me into Elsewhere and makes herself comfortable. She goes off on her own, scratching around the exposed parts of ground between the pews. I relax myself down on the wicker chair and begin the rebirth of my comrades.

Avery should probably be the first since he is the oldest and by default considered the most rotted out. Instead, I start with the three dream commanders. A cap is pulled off. Guts extracted. Oval eyes, triangle nose, pointed down of course, and a mouth that looks like stitches. Zipper is done. Reborn, a phoenix among the gourds. I push the soft decayed Zipper, who sat on the pew next to his fellow churchgoers, to the ground where he busted open a little bit. With a fresh Zipper in his rightful place I then knock Blue and Ghost to the ground in preparation for the arrival of their successors. I grab a blank canvas of squash form and begin knifing a new Blue. Getting halfway into rounding her upside down heart-shaped nose I take notice of the new resident. So immersed in re-carving the pumpkins it seems that I almost forgot about the little bird. She is doing something I find myself quite amused to witness. The remains of my departed trio of dream invaders are being clawed at and eaten by the new addition to this abode of dark charm. Stringy orange brain matter hangs from her beak while she perks up to look at me before going in for more pulp. Her fiendish devouring and claw-ripping emulates that of a monster. And in this moment her name was chosen. I will be calling this feathered hunger-fiend Monster from now on.

The oblong Blue was finished before I knew it and then so was Ghost with his oval mouth of surprise, that I attribute is because of how well these three matched their former selves. Feeling overcome with hunger, I put carving Avery on hold in order to eat. Monster watches me rip off pieces from the bread loaf and scoop out beans from a can with it. She exudes all the familiar symptoms of begging. Staring at my food. Pacing. Light clucking that I interpret as attempting to hold back a demanding squawk. Normally I would not give in to this kind of behavior but I see this all as an experiment to be tested. Good nature plays no part in me; I could just as easily get up, snap her neck and roast her over a fire for dinner and it would make no difference. I pull a few tiny pieces of bread and throw them her way. Monster eagerly pecks them all up in robotic movements. I now tip the can of baked beans out in front of me so a small pile lands by her. Again, she devours this food before going back over to tear through more of the senior Zipper's mushy flesh.

By the time I finish Avery it has already begun to get dark outside. I light the candles for me and Monster, who has now built herself a nest by kicking leaves and twigs from outside through a Monster-sized hole in the church wall. She piled these forest gatherings up under the front pew where Eeka sat; the opposite side of the aisle from the three others. Avery watches over us all while I lay back in my sleeping on the stage and look up at the night sky through openings in the roof. A feeling of contentment washes over me… until I see the first few flakes of snow.

PART TWO

$$-1-$$

Autumn so far has been tiresome and cold. It snowed a few times more that first week after the initial flurry, the day I nabbed Monster. For the past ten days or so after that week, leading up to now, there have been more frequent snow showers. From what I hear it is more snow than usual, but this cold front is expected to pass and get a bit warmer again. Thankfully, the snow spells do not last very long. Preparations must soon be taken to ensure that I will be able to survive through the approaching winter. As much as I hate to get rid of the holes in the roof, I have to patch them up to keep the snow out. Yet another trip into town is underway, this time for a big haul of supplies. I leave Monster behind, as usual, to hold down the fort. She stays relatively close to the church or simply just stays inside of it at all times.

There is always new construction happening in Saint Ox, though because of the season it is becoming a bit more scarce. I drive around scouting out sites to steal building material from and come across two. New homes in separate neighborhoods. I am able to loot much more plywood than the roof repairs call for, as well as roof rolls, a few handfuls of nails, many two-by-fours, a handsaw, hammer, a couple of tarps and drop cloths, and a flannel winter coat in my size. There were also piles of shavings and sawdust from pine trees that were cut down on one of the properties. I loaded up a few five-gallon buckets worth of the stuff to bring back for the little Monster to add to her nest. I also scored the five-gallon buckets from this site. The last thing I was able to take before going back up was a bale of hay from one of the farms on the outskirts of town. I have now successfully maxed out the space in my truck with materials. The only thing I really need to do when I get home is make a natural plaster that some call cob. This is done by mixing dirt and shredded hay with some water. Once it starts to look like drying mud it is left to sit until needed so that all the ingredients bind themselves to each other.

Pumpkins are out of season for this area right now, or all have been sold. It is rare for me now to find one for sale or even to thieve. The last haul I was able to purchase was a good handful of the small blue ones, but that was over a week ago. This is a huge disappointment. I have been keeping all the old rebirths propped up and scattered throughout the pews. They are rotting away but I realized that even in their decomposing state they still have some ambience to add to the place. I have also carved little faces on the small blue ones. These are scattered throughout the different pews in pairs or trios as well. I call them The Ocean, collectively.

What Avery sees when he looks out to his fellowship from his perch is a medley of expressional faces at all different stages of decay and droop. Large white ones are dabbled throughout with the rest of them. All in all, there are around thirty of these jack-o'lanterns on the prayer benches, all facing the stage. At night, when the candles are lit, their faces come to life. The flickering of the wicks causes shadows to move the expressions of their faces against the dim backdrop of the evening church. If I am looking at them from upon the stage I will see each and all moving their mouths as the shadow their openings cast moves around their face. They all silently talk to me like this at the same time, with their dark animated eyes just as spirited as their mouths, making whatever they are saying emphasized and with infliction. The Ocean unsettles me the most as they are all the same size with roughly the same faces, which makes everything they say from the fluttering light exactly the same. A hive mind made of pulp and thin waxy skin. Conveying a mysterious message with their silent voice. Perhaps they are only able to hear each other.

Monster struts around, weaving between the pews of pumpkins looking for bugs and things to scratch at. She is about the only thing that can break my concentration at night from my wicker chair atop the stage looking out and mesmerized by all the babbling heads. Her perplexing movements and whatever makes her tick is enough to make me shift focus from the pumpkins and contemplate. I still have not quite been able to figure Monster out but observing her can occupy my attention for hours on end. I blow out the candles and settle into my sleeping bag on the stage. Monster cozies up in her nest of sticks, leaves and pine shavings underneath Zipper, Blue and Ghost of the front pew.

-2-

I awake bright and early the next morning to get started on repairing the old Church of Elsewhere of any and all flaws that will allow the weather or even the slightest draft in. It is not nearly as cold as some of the more recent mornings and is also warming up faster than usual today. I am hoping this means it will be an especially agreeable temperature because my plan is to start early and have everything finished before the sun starts going back down.

The walls are simple enough. I go around to each hole that burdens the place and nail an appropriately-sized piece of plywood over them on the outside wall. Instead of blocking off the little opening that Monster uses to get in and out of, I remove a mud flap from my truck and fashion it into a flap door for her to push through. The roof was a bit less challenging than I anticipated. Plywood was laid and nailed over all the holes up there. After that I was able to unroll the roofing roll over most of the roof. Then I went around and nailed a couple of two-by-four pieces, over the plywood spots, to the existing beams to lock them in. Nothing about what I just did would be considered professional, but it will surely be functional enough.

When all the wood was set and the hammering was done I moved on to filling the substantial cracks in all the panels to prevent drafts from slipping through. My homemade cob mix of earth, shredded straw and water only took about an hour to plaster to the cracks. This stuff is much better for the aesthetic that I am trying to achieve with the church. It is more natural and old-time looking than anything you can buy from a store and keeps the dark coloring of it as a whole. The stone fireplace and chimney were still mostly intact. I replaced a few stones that probably did not need replacing, but helped the structure look more complete. I tested that there was a clear path for smoke to flow by going back up to the roof and throwing rocks down in addition to poking around with a long branch from the bottom and from the top. No obstructions to be found.

With the remainder of the daylight I chop wood with the axe I stole a few weeks back from the family house in Saint Ox.

Chopping wood will be a chore I give to myself whenever I have free time from now on.

At night sometimes, I try to see if I can induce any sense of dread within myself out here. I think that for most people a place like this would be too terrifying to consider camping at, alone or not. The imagination easily runs wild in a setting like this one. Middle of the woods. Decaying old church. Ravens. All of this during a witchy time of year. But not me. There is very little that ever stirs up a genuine feeling of fear in me anymore. I almost crave it now. When you are young, something as simple as a dark room scares the life out of you. That panic gradually fades away as you get older. For people like me it completely dissolves. Numb to fear and, to be honest, most of the basic emotions that one should still have throughout their life. As I sit outside of the church and look up at the sky and trees this evening, I imagine faces of all different made-up creatures grinning back at me. They do nothing other than gaze in my direction, leaving me to wonder if they are actually plotting something sinister or just being menacing. I let this fantasy go when I realize that I am completely unmoved.

-3-

Now that the task of repairing and winterizing the Elsewhere Church is as complete as I would like, I find it is time to reward myself with another road trip. This time, I make for Vermont. Being where I am in northwestern Massachusetts it is a short drive to the border northward; nearly as close as the New York border is when going west. I continue north about another hour after crossing the state line and need to stop for gas in the city of Elf Cup, Vermont. While not a particularly huge city, Elf Cup still feels substantial when compared to Saint Ox. Not a traditional concrete jungle of a city either, but just the perceived size is big. In fact, with all the lush greenery around and the series of endless woodsy backroads, it has a more welcoming charm than any city I have ever been to. There are also thrift stores and antique shops everywhere around here. I have always heard this about Vermont but did not expect them to be this numerous. Sugar houses, where locals make and sell maple syrup, jams and honey, are prevalent as well.

My back starts to cramp up all of a sudden so I park the truck in an adjacent parking lot of the gas station and take a stroll to stretch my legs. The public library comes into view across the street before I get too far. A stop in here is agreeable to me at the moment, so I enter and start my wanderings through the stacks. I have always enjoyed reading. Of course, there is a liking for fiction, though my fondness for learning about history had led me to choosing it as my minor for studies at college. But today I head straight for the animal husbandry literature.

Within the books of six hundred and thirty-six on the decimal system, a reference book for all things chickens is nestled. After a few minutes of flipping through this book I discover that Monster is, without a doubt, a Belgian breed called Barbu d'Anvers. My suspicion about her age is correct. She is certainly under a year; probably somewhere from six to eight months. Figure I should rip these three pages out of the library book and pocket them for future reference. As I do this, there is a man at the other end of this row of bookshelves that watches me in a disapproving manner. He obviously also wants me to know of his disapproval as he stares me down for a moment with that disgruntled look. This is of no matter to me, I easily convince myself. A person would have to be pretty mental to care about something like that. This style of thinking normally escapes me but is curiously welcomed at the moment.

On my way out of the Elf Cup public library there sits the objective man at the bench beside the glass swinging doors. He wears the same critically disgruntled look on his face as he did inside and he points it right in my direction as I walk by. I am surprised by how much restraint I show. Not only show, but genuinely feel. Historically, I would have made a remark at the very least or may have even attempted some sort of physical harm to this man. Instead, I keep walking; mostly uncharacteristically unfazed. As I approach my truck in the vacant parking lot next to the gas station, ready to continue on my way, I realize this man is following me about twenty paces behind.

At this moment he shouts over to me, "You like stealing from libraries, Mississippi?"

I am now instantly annoyed. I had every intention of letting all the stare-downs go, which I would not ordinarily do. This man is intentionally pushing my buttons and I am frustrated for giving him a pass in the first place. My known instincts should have been fed to start with and now I am angry with myself for letting it get this far. For letting this varmint pursue me so much. This man that I have allowed to act this way towards me only led to him thinking that I am capable of nothing. I should have dealt with him in the library, but did not because it genuinely did not ruffle my feathers. It should have. I should have let them feel ruffled. Then I let him off the hook again while walking out of the library. Again, I should not have. He must want this to escalate deep down. No one would wait outside like that and then proceed to follow someone to their car if they were not ready for an altercation. But, you never know. People are stupid. For instance, how can someone in the perceived safety of their car know what kind of person they are about to cut off is? They may be totally crazy and you are there potentially giving them the final push to do something more irrational than you are. Would it not be smarter and more safe to just assume everyone is capable of doing wicked things in retaliation? For me, I typically stay in a state of always being ready to do something irrational. It saves time that way. Always primed to receive that final push. I lost sight of this somehow today. Does this mean I was becoming a better person or just a weaker one?

"I like to mind my own business," I shout back at him without turning around, then continue with, "because I never know what I'll get myself into if I meddle into things that have nothing to do with me."

I am now approaching the back of my off-blue truck. I have given a few quick turns at this point to really clock how fast he is walking. The man has noticeably picked his pace up and now has an extremely aggressive demeanor. He is marginally taller than me and more stocky, like he possibly frequents the gym. His head is shaved down bald and looks to be in his thirties.

"Ay!" he says, quick and sharp as one of his claws grips my shoulder.

Luckily, as he is initiating violence I was able to grab the hammer from the open window of my truck bed and swing around to bash him once in the head with it. I did not hit him with the claw part or the striking part, but rather the side of those parts, the profile of the tool. He dropped to the pavement without the need for any further hits. I still found it necessary to forcefully kick him in the gut handful of times. He was out cold.

If anyone has ever been more deserving of being taken to my
church of pumpkins then I have not found or harmed them yet.

He is heavier and sturdier than Eeka was to load into the
truck. I wrestle different ways to get him in, but the awkward
way that worked best was grabbing one of his wrists while I
climb up into the covered truck bed. Now that I am up and have
a hold on him I can pull him up further with both hands. First
his arm and shoulder is hoisted. Then, in a headlock, I can lean
back to get his chest and belly onto the tailgate. Easier now just
to hold both his wrists and walk backwards until he is all the
way in. I drop down next to him, out of breath in a sitting
position. I seize my ether inhaler and take a quick couple of
huffs for myself before attaching the face strap to him. Before
climbing out, I make sure to top off the sponges in the glass
with ether to ensure he gets the full experience and stays
unconscious.

I stop at the gas station to use the restroom and purchase
a mini book from the Elf Cup Tourism rack that contains facts
and town history.

No need to hang around here, I figure. Still plenty of
daylight to get home to.

-4-

To my troubled surprise I see that it has snowed since leaving
on my road trip. There are a few powdery inches on the ground
and still some light flurries coming down from the grey
heavens. Monster does not mind the knocked out guest that I
have dragged in. She stays cozied up in her nest under the front

pew of jack-o'lanterns. It is not terribly dark yet, just shaded from the dim sky. I light the candles all the same. The ether mask has been off of our edgy visitor since before removing him from the truck. I force feed him a good heap of those Spanish fly pills I picked up from the gas station weeks ago. I had to do this while he was still out because it is doubtful he would take these willingly, without a fight, were he to be presented with them while conscious. My aim here is nothing of a sexual nature. This is purely experimental to see what happens when someone takes this much of the cantharidin chemical harvested from those particular beetles that they cram into these capsules. With tons of electrical tape, he is bound. I anticipate a fair amount of resistance to the situation from him.

When he finally comes to, there is understandably a great deal of confusion. The eye on the left side of his head, where the welt from the hammer blow is, winces a bit as he tries to make sense of his surroundings. He recognizes me, sitting right in front of him on the wicker throne, looking down from the stage to his pew. He wriggles and jerks with alarmed anger to try and escape the adhesive bindings that trap him.

"It's no use. I used almost two rolls," I calmly explain to him.

"What...the fuck is all this? You know I'm going to kill you for this, right?"

"Other way around, friend. You couldn't mind your business, could you? You tried to intimidate a complete stranger and it backfired, didn't it?"

"You sucker punched me with whatever the fuck you grabbed from your truck. I was going to beat the shit out of you for destroying that book and being an arrogant fuck. My wife works at that library, ya know. She has to deal with punk kids causing all kinds of problems and I was finally able to help get even because an actual grown man pulled some shit there."

"Spare me," I start with as I plan to go on and lecture him about not trying to threaten potentially dangerous people.

He coughs up blood before I can really ramp up to anything inspired. I hold my breath in hopes that his coughing fit was not leading up to vomiting out all the Spanish fly he unknowingly ingested. This was not the case and I am relieved. When he is finished coughing and begins to catch his breath, Monster pops herself out from under the pew next to his. He does not notice her at first as she walks over to me, probably hoping for some kind of food. When he does finally detect her he lets out a little jump then becomes irate all over again with squirming. It is hard to explain how and why exactly I am so utterly bothered by this man. I cannot seem to shake the feeling that it is because he did not give me a choice in letting the whole situation go. He pushed me to this and whatever it is that will happen to him now.

I think I am beginning to see a difference in what I sincerely want when engaging in musings like this and what I do not want. The enjoyment comes from the drive to do the things I do, not from doing them out of frustration and impatience and rage. There is not nearly as much pleasure when those things are involved. There is a sense of satisfaction, sure, but strictly from quelling aggravation. I would much prefer to be only driven to act by the drive itself. Much like it was with Eeka. But if this man insists on wrath then I will have to oblige. I hope to take my time with him, too.

Still writhing on his bench, as if it makes a difference, he begins to shout at me.

With his darkening red face he screams, "Fuck you! Fuck you! I will kill you! Did you drug me while I was

unconscious or something? My fucking mouth," he stops for a
second to vomit more blood, "burns like fire and my stomach
feels like I swallowed a damn train spike!"

Monster is now uneasy. I get up and give the man a few
good punches to the face and one to the welt on his temple. This
tranquilizes him from the massive shouting fit. Before he gets
back to screaming I have the idea to drag him outside behind the
church in the snow. I give him one more thump to the head
before pushing his bound self to the ground. It seems the
Spanish fly poison is taking control. As I pull him down the
church aisle between the pews he talks gibberish about the
pumpkins looking straight ahead with rotted distortion. This
happens in between little bouts of spewing blood.

The only complete thought I can make out of him is,
"The blue fucks are the worst," as we are nearing the door.

I simply cut him off saying, "Mind The Ocean,
asshole."

I am once again out of breath from hauling this man. In
the snow, behind the church, is where I leave him for a moment
while I go and put my stolen construction site flannel on and
grab a few candle stands with lit candles. This helps with the
impending darkening as it shifts into night. It is still lightly
snowing so I may have to drag us both back inside soon.
Hopefully the cold dampens his constitution because I will not
deal with this furious verve of his all night. His state is
declining as he lays on his back in the snow with feet and legs
wrapped together by the electrical tape; hands, wrists and arms
wrapped up as well. He talks quietly and nonsensically to
himself while I go and get the ether. I pour some on a rag and
hold it over his breathing cavities. Just enough time to get high
and spacey but not long enough to knock him out. His
movements become more flowing than erratic, like they just

were. Curious to what he would do with his hands in this state, I go ahead and cut his arms and hands loose. He flows rockingly back and forth as if vibing on the snowy floor to some jam band. He gives small jolts arising from his stomach like he wants to vomit more but does not. His arms reach up over his head into untouched snow. Now they spread from side to side and move back up to extend above his head. A sloppy snow angel is beginning to form from his cursory movements. He shivers a bit and begins very quietly speaking the same thing over and over.

He whispers, "Fuck you. Fuck you. Fuck you," until his voice gradually gets louder. "Fuck you. Fuck!… you. Fuck you!"

Monster comes strutting out around back with us. She must have left through her little mudflapped Monster door to check up on us. She gives a few sporadic head tilts of acknowledgment and goes about scratching around in the snow under the roof eave where it is most shallow.

The man continues to get louder and angrier sounding, "Fuck you! Fuck! You! Fuck you!"

My patience with him has nearly run out. Nothing about this is pleasurable and I cannot get his threatening manner from earlier out of my mind. I walk closer to him and he manages to lift his taped legs up and strongly kick me directly in the chest. I am stunned and storming on the inside. His movements are still quite fluid and wavy and the snow angel is looking much more proper now as he is keeping his arms straight. They move from his sides to the top of his head consistently. The familiar puking of blood has resumed in full force. A few times to his left side and a few to his right. Blood-soaked snow all around his head. His shouting stops when he retches but then returns again at full force, which is continuing to make all of this an agitated, unpleasant scene for me. I ether him again quickly and he breaks his shouting spell for a moment, before starting again in a loud but slurring manner.

"Fluhhhck looo!"

I've tried everything I could try and it is cold out. I reach for the axe that is leaning up against the church and bring it down on the left wrist of the poisoned man. This hand was halfway from coming down on its snow angel route; outstretched horizontally from him as if beckoning someone for a hug. The axe strikes true and his hand comes clean off with a faint popping sound as it happens. He barks out, loudly, all kinds of unintelligible words. His arms continue the motions, almost unhindered. One side is trailing blood to stain the snow and the other side stays mostly unmarked and pure. That is, until I walk up to the top of him and cut the other hand off as it reaches the highest point above his head. He continues the repetitive angel motions with his handless limbs in the snow a few more times and then stops. I stand over him at his hips. One of my legs on one side of his hips and the other leg on the other side. I almost wish he would try and kick me again, but he does not. I hate that I want a reason to get more upset.

This man is overly poisoned. He will not survive much longer anyway. I raise the axe far above and behind my head just as when I am about to chop through a piece of wood. I bring it down swiftly. The sharp blade lands precisely in the center of his face. His nose is split. His forehead is split. Mouth is split. Teeth and jaw are split; fragments of bone and tooth fly out. Blood pours out and further soaks the snow. I am tired and disappointed. Unfulfilled. I leave the axe buried inside the man's hewed face and turn in for the night. Monster enters unvexed by this incident a few moments after me through the

Monster door and goes to her nest. I light us a fire in the stone fireplace on the stage and we sleep.

-5-

My stomach is repeatedly lifted lightly then dropped with a rush like I am on a rollercoaster. When my vision comes into focus it appears I have ended up in a basement of some kind, possibly during an earthquake. No, that cannot be right. Now I know. I am in the lower deck of a ship. The air is a bit fuzzy, yet slightly glowing at the same time. I start to become aware in my confusion of the situation, but quickly remember a mantra.

Being confused is okay. Panicking about confusion could be catastrophic. Just go with it.

It is damp and dark and made of wood where I am. A row of historic cannons are beside me, casually poking their firing ends out from rope-opened windows. My stomach drops again as this moving ship crashes down from another hefty ocean wave. The gunport part of the vessel I am in is astoundingly large. There are many wooden barrels filled with gunpowder and sturdy crates next to each of the mounted cannons with iron cannonballs inside.

I still have enough of the fading daylight outside that pushes through the artillery windows to give me sufficient ambient light for seeing. I discover more crates with foodstuff in them. Lots of cured and dried meats, beans, apples and other fruits, bread, cabbage and things of the like. Randomly leaned up against walls are long curved swords along with antiquated rifles or muskets.

From what I can see, while sticking my head out of one of the windows, it seems as though I am aboard an enormous olden frigate-style ship; one of those warships one would see in old swashbuckler films. When I pull myself back into the hull there stands a familiar shadowy figure wearing off-white and billowy cotton garments with a well worn black leather corset, held together with tarnished golden clasps. My legs feel flimsy all of a sudden. The woman comes into view, but my vision is murky. I now recognize her, but can barely get the sense of who I am. Her hair, now more in focus, has gone from the familiar brown to a much darker brown, almost black. I try not to think about this too much in order to keep confusion at bay.

Eeka steps closer and says, "Go," with a soft voice while pointing her finger and eyes towards a sizable staircase leading up.

I have the feeling of wanting to reply but I cannot see the point in it. The waves rebound upon the ship with great force causing an even greater thunderous sound.

I am buried up to my neck in sand. I am okay with this. I am back on the sailing vessel, ascending the stairs.

A few paces up the creaky wooden steps before I sense as though someone is watching me. I stop mid step and turn around to see three pumpkin-headed forms. The creepily embodied Zipper, Blue and Ghost have manifested and returned to me once again. Their attire has changed, from the ragged grey suits I last beheld them in, to khaki colored linen shirts with laced chests and loose fitting dark tan breeches. We all stand silent for a few moments. Me, in slight awe of once more getting to witness the pumpkin-faced humanoid chimeras. Them, with their now somewhat rotted drooped faces holding a serious glare on me.

Blue steps forward to break the tension and says in a lowish yet feminine voice, "Resurrector of ours, you must speak with the captain."

The sagging of her mouth as she speaks is too inhuman not to fixate on. It has the slumping motion of a face made from malleable clay.

"Captain?" I ask in a long drawn out cadence.

Another heavy slam into the ocean occurs and I almost lose my footing on the stairs.

Zipper now steps up next to Blue and tells me, "The captain will explain. We have told him everything. Go, speak with the captain. Attend this command at once."

Their faces all droop a little bit more, simultaneously, causing them to deepen their dreadfully serious stares. Ghost starts walking towards me with his once unthreatening face, now turned to a haunting gape, and does not stop advancing in my direction. This unstoppable imposing gesture is meant to give me no option but to turn around and walk up the stairs. Which I promptly do when I realize that Ghost will not halt this marching until I move.

Emerging into the top deck does not make the atmosphere much brighter, even though I am now under the open sky. The fuzzy glow around enhances and makes things more visible than the hull below, but grey still rules the visual mood and skies.

I am somewhere surrounded by fire. Dark flames all around me but I am not overheating. I am back on the upper deck of the flameless ship.

Multiple masts behind and before me extend straight up as tall as I can discern. Tanned dirty sails of different sizes puff out from each of them, making the vessel exceedingly more profound to me. The ratlines of knotted and networked rope that lead up to the crows nests, atop the masts, hold taught and impressive through every startling collision the ship makes with each wave. There are no other beings on the old ship as far as I can see.

Just go with it. Do not wonder who or if anyone is guiding this massive sailing craft. Everything is fine.

I turn and look to the back of the boat. I can see the quarterdeck; this being another raised deck with stairs leading up to it on both sides. The wheel for steering is just barely visible from my viewpoint. I can also tell that there is no one manning this helm. Between the two staircases that ascend to this stern is a large doorway with stairs that lead down. I presume this is the captain's quarters and where I am intended to go.

I walk down the stairs and they take me to a large thick wooden door with a heavy iron ring handle. My head has almost no thoughts running through it at this point. I am on autopilot while boldly grabbing the iron hoop with both hands and then a pull. A smokey room presents itself. Dark red tapestries and rugs dress the candlelit commander's chamber. Nautical devices and tools accompany the jugs of wine and rum on the skillfully chiseled tables of artful design. While still damp and sullen like the rest of the ship, this room has a saving mitigating fiber to it. I have not lost my muddled frame of mind but have begun a growing hope that my mental perception will clear up and become cognitive. There is no way of working out how to cultivate this hope, though. Only to let it sit and linger without approaching it.

Do not dwell on this realization. Everything is as it should be. It has to be.

There are paintings in antique frames hung on the walls with no real images. Just different colored paint streaks and blotches. A few mirrors are also scattered around. I do not take any kind of close look at either of these. Relic swords and firearms also occupy the wall space. These are much more ornamental than the ones in the gunport.

In my ongoing bewilderment inside the captain's quarter I almost do not notice the captain himself approaching me from the side. At a few steps away I slowly turn to see the stout man of medium height that one might stereotype as a sea captain. His paled and well worn red coat was open and of full length, all the way to his shins. Embellished with chipped and partially rusted gold clips and hooks, it looked far less distinguished than it most certainly once was at some point in time. A ruffled cloth neckerchief was pulled off from around his neck in an attempt at comforting relief. A thick silken shirt of navy blue underneath his coat jutted out down to his thighs. His legs wore black breeches that were not quite as baggy as the ones those pumpkin bipeds had on. All of this, while having an overly underwhelming prestige that might be expected in a captain, was conventional.

His head, on the contrary, was most deviantly abnormal. The entire face and head is smooth and a deep blue color. Almost the same shade as his silken shirt. There are white arabesque patterns of sharp but flowery vine-like shapes all around his face. The eyes and eyebrows are fixed in an angered demeanor that is only accentuated by the furrowing brow. The only feature that makes me question his disgruntlement is the slight smirk he wears on his mouth. With this in the facial equation it makes the whole guise seem menacing and calculating rather than hostile. His nose is long and sticks straight out from his head just over the length of a finger. It is thick and rounded at the end. I am reminded of those faces and masks of Japanese folklore, the tengu demon beings.

Another wave smacks the moving ship and the candles flicker wildly for a moment. The tension in the room reaches all different highs and lows of intensity while light shifts and then resumes to the normal tenor.

"Your three legion have communicated to me some things I would like to relay to you," he says in a powerfully emotionless voice.

He continues, "We have struck a deal in order to make your work more intentional. They will back off a bit, not completely, but enough for you to actualize your journey to yourself. For yourself. By yourself. To continue your becoming and nourish the seed of your true unhindered spirit. Their current decaying state cannot be helped and they understand this. Become more than what you are and remember my face."

I stare at him dreamingly but with total regard. I am still taken with his bizarre features, but listening intently all the same. I cannot claim to be able to make heads or tails of his words at this moment. He realizes this though. I just know it.

"You may not understand what I am saying but this is of no consequence. Now go. You must leave here and return home. We are finished."

For the entire time I have been in his presence the features on his face have not shifted. They are completely fixed except for his mouth as it moves when he speaks. His face is no mask but it may as well be functioning as one.

I begin walking out of the tengu captains quarters and up the stairs. I am faced with wondering what he meant by me leaving here and returning home. Am I not home? I have almost no memory of anything before or outside of this ship. There is a familiarity with things here that I feel goes beyond my limited memory, but it is only a feeling.

Become more and remember his face? Why?

Do not get confused. Just go with it. Keep walking and take things moment to moment.

When I get back to the upper deck and open air I am met with the three pirate-like embodied pumpkins. They are towards the side of the boat by one of the staircases leading up to the stern.

Now standing close to the railing at the bottom of these ascending steps, Ghost, with his sad mushy openings, vocalizes to me, "Resurrector. No resurrection is possible without surrogates being born to create us. We understand and accept this, for the time being. You will go home now. We will be your ushers."

Another wave collides with the ship and a mighty wave is both heard and seen erupting from where I am now standing. Just the sound of this triggers the three to spring to action with alarming agility that I feel I have seen once before. Ghost shoots forwards and wraps his arm around my neck, effectively securing me in a headlock. Zipper and Blue go low with the same charging initiative and take hold of one leg each. As they carry me those few steps closer to the railing with my back to the ground and eyes to the sky, I briefly get a glimpse of a figure up in the crow's nest. I believe this to be Eeka, looking down at the event happening below her. I am struggling to break free from my detainers. This is the most amount of energy I can recall ever exerting at the moment. They are incredibly strong and I have to now accept that whatever it is they are planning I cannot fight it.

Just go with it.

In unison they all lift and shove me from their grasps over and out from the boat, just clearing the railing. I am now freed from the powerful restraints that I was helpless to break away from on my own accord. Now falling with my back to those waves that will certainly swallow me in an instant. I am facing up and see Zipper, Blue and Ghost who are looking down at the creator they have cast out. They then turn to leave before they can even witness the grand finale. Right before I sense the collision I am about to make, I look over my shoulder below me. It is an endless sea of infinite small blue pumpkins with faces all pointing at me. The ocean. The Ocean. I hold my breath and brace for impact and...

I expel a huge mass of air from my chest as I open my eyes. Out of breath and turned sideways on the church stage towards the room of pumpkins. Monster sits perked up and watches me from her nest underneath the front pew. I roll in the other direction to now face the fireplace. The flames have gone out but there are many hot coals still smoldering.

It is morning and a lazy one at that. The intense dream I had sucked the rest of the vigor from me that had not already been taken by the dissatisfaction of last night's uninspired execution. I roll up the sleeping bag and stash it next to the fireplace before taking a seat in the wicker chair. A French press of coffee and some instant oatmeal helps me recover from the dream, which I am now writing down in my journal before I lose it. I sip the coffee and throw little handfuls of my oatmeal to Monster. So far, I have not found any other food that is more enjoyable to her. I should start considering a proper diet for the tiny Monster, but this thought only lasts a short moment before I begin thinking about the task of cleaning last night's disheartening mess.

The man outside is exactly where I butchered and left him. His severed hands still lay half clenched near his body. There is a thin dusting of snow blanketing the corpse but not obscuring it much. Seeing this image in the morning light is in direct contrast to the hectic atmosphere of last night. It is calm and tranquil. I leisurely start to pull on the axe handle in an attempt to remove its sharp bit from his split face. It requires much muscle since all I am achieving is lifting his forked head up along with the cleaving tool. A wiggle, push and tug releases the business end from the man's broken face. From his chin to his forehead there is now a cleft opening. A slow bit of chilled blood rolls out, along with a lump of brain falling to the center of the gory facial crevice. His lifeless faded eyes rest in an almost crossed way. Reddish pink snow encircles the top half of his body in a rather uniform filled-in ring.

I am sick of looking at this unpleasant man. I have to let of go the frustration he had caused, starting with his refusal to just go about his business at the Elf Cup library. If I cannot focus on other things right now then I will waste more time mangling him further. Instead, I drag him out into the snowy forest for almost an hour. I am met with the challenge of digging a grave in exceptionally cold earth. The spade meets with much more of a firm resistance than it did when digging the hole for Eeka. Fortunately, it is not consistently frozen ground as it still tends to warm up enough during the day. Digging a hole is much like chopping wood. I can let go of anything on my mind and the act itself becomes an unfocused meditation. I pull the body up parallel next to the hole and take the money from his wallet before I push him in. A thud sound occurs when it lands face down in this final resting spot. He is then buried. Good riddance.

Monster has made her way out to come look for me as I near Elsewhere, coming from the burial in the woods. She is just past the bloody site from last night. I take a moment to admire this scene. For all of the trouble that yesterday has caused me I can honestly say that what remains is a captivating image. The bodiless snow angel is a deep red color at the center where the imprint of his head was. It gradually lightens in tint to a soft pink the further out you go from the arms-length circle. I see no blood outside of the perfect circle ending at the hips. Just a straight and narrow mould of white legs protruding down. Monster instinctually scratches the snow and dirt behind me looking for bugs or seeds to eat as I continue to take in this work of art. Just then I note a couple of objects that did not make it with me on the journey into the woods, but may make for a few decent decorations in the church.

I had forgotten to bury the hands.

-6-

To take my mind off of the past day I make the choice to educate myself on the city of Elf Cup. Might as well get something positive from the experience and escape into learning. History has always been a suitable distraction for me. I retrieve the book I bought from the Elf Cup tourist rack at the gas station and sit by the fireplace in the Elsewhere Church. A small fire is lit and I crack open the book.

I learn that Elf Cup was named after a type of mushroom of the same name. It can be found all over the region. Prior to being titled Elf Cup in the year nineteen twenty-one it was called Brewer. Brewer derived the name from having deep roots with brewing beer and distributing it to the public since the mid seventeen-hundreds, until the Vermont government passed its own form of prohibition at the very tail end of the seventeen-hundreds. This restricted the selling and overall manufacturing of alcohol throughout the state. Despite the laws forbidding this, these beer makers continued brewing and selling the product in an underground fashion. The government remained fully aware of the huge disregard of the law in Brewer and made it a cardinal mission to eradicate any of these lawbreakers, by any means necessary. Tactics for putting a stop to the individuals included mild approaches like warnings, fines and arrests. Much like the moonshiners of Appalachia during the national prohibition of years later, this did not stop the brewers from brewing. It only inclined inventiveness for finding ways around being caught. With beer still being made in great abundance the government took to harsher strategies. Fires were set to people's property that were even suspected of producing alcohol. Lawmen were instructed to discreetly beat those who were found to be breaking these laws, with some occurrences resulting in death. Threats were made. Lives were ruined. Foul play from officers and officials ran rampant towards those who were ignoring this decree. This all led up to a series of events that was nearly lost in history and hidden by those who perpetrated it. The incidents of this time are known as The Brewmen's Torment. This lasted only two months. Nearly all of the people brewing during Vermont's prohibition were men. The women did not have much business in all the dealings surrounding their male counterparts. Occasionally, you might see one of the wives transporting the outlawed substances or a daughter collecting money for their father, but other than that they were minding not to get involved. Those who were protecting and enforcing the laws saw this as a weakness in the peddlers' defenses.

This was not too long after the mass hysteria of witchcraft cases in New England. It had died down quite a bit to almost non-existing, but witch accusations did still pop up. At this point in history there were many written and rewritten statements and bills formed regarding witchcraft that changed the public's outlook on things. This still did not stop incidents with witch trials showing up well into the eighteen-hundreds. Vermont had nearly none of these cases and trials involving witches at this point in history. It was Massachusetts that held the big numbers for these affairs in the past. While the beer brewers kept finding new ways to keep the upper hand in the war against Vermont prohibition, the state was doing the same and their next move was going to be a callous one.

The wives, daughters, sisters, girlfriends, mothers and any form of affectatious relationship with a female by the alcohol trafficking menfolk were marked as agents of witchcraft. The paranoia of yesteryear had once again emerged in Brewer, Vermont. With the government being the ones pioneering these witch hunts there was very little the bootleggers could do to stop it. A woman would be accused and arrested. From there anyone who could not see past the ploy that was actually happening had turned against the accused. This was mostly anyone who was not involved in the beer racket. The turning was out of fear and public pressure, the same devices that are used to control people to this day. The women were held for days and days before being allowed to even speak with anyone outside of the jail. When their male redeemer was finally allowed to see the innocent females it was obvious they had been bested. Their lives were not worth sacrificing for beer. Some men held out longer than others in an attempt to call this potential bluff, but once the beatings started on the women and children it was time to give up their ways. Female loved ones were miraculously found innocent of being witches and released in all different conditions, but alive. Slowly and surely over the next two months the beer flow had been stomped out. The government had nearly won now.

There was one last man who would not secede from his illegal trade in order to have his young wife liberated. He spoke with her every day that he could and they shared stories from their current situations; his from the outside world and hers on the inside. She was beaten regularly and he kept brewing while people kept buying, knowing full well they were contributing to her situation. The wife was eventually told that if she were to be found guilty at her trial she would be executed. Given a witches death. Her other half did not quit standing his ground despite his spouse's pleas. A simple request in her eyes; stop brewing beer to save her life. The husband did not show up to the trial. His wife knew this would be the case as her husband told her so. He would be staying away and getting blind drunk off of his own beer. She was indeed found guilty and to be executed at midnight the very same evening.

The townspeople went home after the trial and went about their business. They ate dinner, gossiped and prepared themselves to witness the killing of a condemned witch.

A rope was tied high up on the thick limb of a large half-dead red maple tree at the Brewer community gathering hill. A shabby staircase was built leading up to this branch with a platform for standing at the top. Underneath this tree branch was a hefty fire pit with a bounty of firewood organized inside. At nearly midnight, the guilty was marched up the ladder. She looked out unto the crowd of people she knew so well. Neighbors, friends and family. People she had known and happily coexisted with for most of her life. All there to watch her die, without objection. Her husband being the only face that was not in the swarm of peers, as well as the only one that could liberate her. The rope was slipped around her neck as she stood at the top of the high platform.

She announces, "I may die now… but I will live on in the elf cups. That is where you will find me."

The crowd had stood quietly and watched as the executioner walked up the last few steps to push her. Before he could get that far the woman had jumped. The rope snapped tight and the knot of the noose did what it was intended to do. That is, provide an instant death by having the knot placed just behind the ear in order to swiftly make impact with the spinal cord. She had swung, dead. The immense fire was lit at once. It built up to a rage with haste. The clothes on the hanging body above it were then beginning to catch on fire and engulf the woman. As the flames worked their way up to her chest and shoulders the rope around her neck began to burn and come undone. When finally it broke open she fell, with dead weight, into the bonfire. Most trials that end in an execution of this caliber are either burned or hanged, but never both. There are many theories for the reason behind this but most have settled on that it was simply to make an extreme statement. She burned with the fire throughout the night. All alone.

The remains of the woman were eventually collected and buried in an unknown location. There was not much to gather by the time the fire quit smoldering two days later. Most of her matter now belonged under the big red maple tree. Over the following months and years that tree continued to die and fall apart where it stood. The leftover debris was never moved. Other trees and vegetation grew up around it while its branches and trunk decayed. Mushrooms eventually made a home on this wood and earth. Elf cups grew in great abundance here. Eventually the spores from these elf cups made their way all over Brewer and the town had become a haven for the spreading fungi fruit.

Sixteen years after the finale of rope and fire at the era of The Brewmen's Torment the Vermont government had lifted the law of prohibition. Beer was legal once more to brew and sell. The story of the hanged and burned woman who was made an example of and took the fall for her peddler husband, and the whole town of Brewer if you look at it that way, was scrubbed from history by the government and the town. Erased, forgotten and never spoken about. Until just over a hundred years later. In nineteen-twenty the national prohibition law went into effect. It was at this time that a diary was discovered and released from a house in Brewer. This belonged to that guilty innocent woman. It told of everything that had happened in Brewer from the beginning of Vermont's prohibition and the effect on the town; the events that occurred from all sides of the struggle between government and brewers. All the facts were there, leading up to the night of her execution.

This part of forgotten history immediately became a thing of local legend. Then, from piecing together stories passed down to the townsfolk, and other old journals and letters, it left legend status and became historical fact. The woman was referred to as The Brewer Witch from then on. When people use this term it is meant as more of an endearing title, rather than a malicious one. The information in her journal was used to show the dangers of these kinds of laws and how quickly they can get out of control. The United States government, along with the Vermont one were now backed into a corner of information they could not deny. It changed nothing in regards to the laws prohibiting alcohol. But in an effort to cover their tracks and erase ties to their alcohol-riddled past, the town of Brewer took a vote to change the name. Most were eager for this change of name. The voting process leaned in favor of honoring the woman they had forgotten about for over a century. The town was renamed Elf Cup. This was appropriate on another level as the elf cup growth in the town had grown to overwhelming proportions. They were everywhere. Even as the town grew into a city the elf cups still dominated the forests and fields.

Thirteen years after the United States era of prohibition was launched it had come to an end. Nineteen thirty-three was the year everyone came out from the shadows and drank their spirits publicly. The spirit of The Brewer Witch lives on in Elf Cup, Vermont through the elf cups that populate it. These mushrooms that look like little red cupped saucers are eaten and sold by the townspeople. Because of the mass quantities of these mushrooms that grow around Elf Cup the city has two annual Elf Cup Festivals a year. The semi-annual events are held in winter and spring. Here, the locals vend various elf cup mushroom edibles such as infused honey, salads that include other native forages, fried elf cups, pizzas topped with them, stews and soups, stuffed elf cups with all kinds of ingredients, jars of pickled elf cups and shots of the mushroom infused liquor from the cups themselves. They apparently do not mention or cash in on the story of The Brewer Witch in the city of Elf Cup at these festivals or outside of them the way that Salem, Massachusetts does with their historic witch trials, for example. The people who know the history tend to keep it to themselves. Yet, they are reminded of the mushroom martyr woman who offered her death to the fungal ecosystem of the town that betrayed her. With every bite of the scarlet flesh that she proclaimed to resurrect inside of, they remember her tale.

Tomorrow is Halloween. I would like to make up for my last slaughter in an immense way.

PART THREE

-1-

All Hallows Eve. In the morning I prepare a monumental breakfast in comparison to the meals I usually make since moving here. I foresee needing all the energy and vitality I can possibly get for when I go out this evening. It has been much easier to keep food since the weather turned cold. The meal consists of five eggs, a large bowl of oatmeal with sliced honeycrisp apples, two fried ham slices, a few pieces of toasted bread thanks to the leftover coals from the fireplace, instant grits and coffee. I was also fortunate to notice some sassafras saplings when I went out to urinate before starting on breakfast. The unmistakable leaves with three well rounded points hung from the saplings at knees-length and were almost hit with my stream. I was once told that the leaves look like dinosaur feet. This is what I always think of when remembering how to identify sassafras. I dug up two of these sapling roots and boiled them into a tea, which tastes like smooth licorice with a hint of vanilla.

      This morning is much warmer than it has been lately. The snow has melted and I can once again see all the dead leaves on the forest floor. The blood angel has dissolved into the earth.

I eat my breakfast outside at the front of the church to enjoy this unexpectedly mild morning weather. Monster joins me, as usual whenever I am eating. She successfully begs for food throughout the whole meal. Bits of bread, scrambled eggs and oats are dropped for her that she readily pecks up. I am fairly sure that she stole some bits of ham off my plate when I walked over to fetch salt and pepper from the truck. When I am finished eating I go ahead and clean up. Then I remind myself to grace Elsewhere with the new ornaments collected from that unpleasant man. The hands are nailed straight through the palm to the front of the podium, side by side and completely open. I hope they stay outstretched this way. It gives me a sense of conciliated sensibility. Whereas envisioning a clenched hand or a fist on there makes me start to feel a sense of edginess.

The audience of pumpkins arranged throughout the church still appears drooping and glum. When I consider what day it is, Halloween, I can accept this morose disposition of their features and picture them coming alive with an anxious spirit that is ready for mayhem.

I still have some time before my planned time of departure, so to make use of it I get up on the roof and fix the steeple to the best of my ability. As of right now, it is the most well put-together part of the church. I figure that when it comes to the restoration I will start from the top and work my way down the structure; and hopefully not lose the moody essence of this place in the process.

I make sure to take everything I might possibly need, including the jar of LSD tabs, with me before I depart for my holiday romp.

I drove straight down from the Elsewhere Church and kept going until I was in Connecticut. The autumn foliage is exactly as expected from the pictures I have seen throughout my life. Up in my mountains the leaves have all already died and fallen due to it being so much colder in the higher elevation. Here, the orange, browns and yellows remain lively clinging to the trees that squeezed them out. There are even patches of green left to be seen on the almost endless expanse of treetops in every viewable direction from the highway. I am looking forward to the exit off the freeway that I am about to take so I can see the towns up close and begin my devilry.

The covered wooden bridges and old historic houses that pop up throughout this region add to the aesthetic of the colonial heritage that I am so drawn to. I arrived aimlessly in the town of Cornham. The townspeople have leaned heavily into the Halloween spirit. All of the houses are donned with spooky decorations of cobwebs and black cats. The pumpkin season must span longer in these parts compared to the Saint Ox region. Jack-o'-lanterns are placed on nearly all of the steps and porches of the Georgian and Dutch colonial homes that blanket Cornham. The downtown and city center districts have streets of dark cobblestone. Buildings for the various businesses are well kept structures at least a few hundred years old. They stand two to three stories tall and most are all connected to each other leaving the occasional back alley here or there between the ones that are not. Black and orange streamers sway from windows and vintage lamp posts. Skulls are ornamented on each spout of the large elaborate fountain at the common area of the town green. Banners hang across the roads above streetlights promoting the townwide celebration this evening and the Harrowing Parade at midnight. I feel as though this is exactly where I am meant to be at this moment in time. There is still

some light left in the day to get bearings of my surroundings in
Cornham. I make sure to go beyond each corner of the town to
find a suitable camping spot, should I need to spend the night. It
seems this will not be a problem as there are stretches of
woodsy areas in all directions.

When darkness starts to curtain the sky I leave the
wooded spot I have designated as my potential last minute
camping space and head for where the action is. I park many
blocks away from the town green and walk there, as this is
where the celebration is about to start. I made it just in time for
the sun to be fully set. The Cornham mayor stands on the edge
of that big fountain I spotted here earlier and announces a
speech through the microphone he holds. A sea of people in
scary or sultry costumes pipe down while they look and listen to
what he has to say in the moonlit atmosphere.

"Good evening people of Cornham and visitors to our
town! Welcome to the nineteen ninety-seven Halloween
festival!" he says proudly and the crowd erupts in a clang of
clapping, cheering and ghoulish noises.

"I am pleased to kick things off by letting you know the
park has filled every vendor spot this year, so you have many
options for food, entertainment or shopping. Support your
community by visiting all the unique stands that the Cornham
Halloween Festival has to offer and don't forget to stick around
until the witching hour of midnight for the Harrowing Parade!
This is sure to be a Halloween to remember."

I could not agree more with that last part.

The costumed crowd breaks off in all different
directions of the festival grounds. A group of grey-faced bloody
zombies makes for the long row of food stands. A few slutty
angels go towards the bar across the street from the park.
Children in ghost and vampire and pumpkin costumes drag their

parents this way and that. And the whole array of dressed up celebrants create a tide of directionless movement that pushes through one another. I sink myself into the waves of the dead and sexy and toothy. I pass vikings hosting hatchet-throwing into pumpkins, pirates selling chances to win different pieces of junk depending on which black balloon you pop with a dart and adult schoolgirls prostituting themselves with lipstick-covered kisses on the cheek in exchange for money.

One large velvety claret-red tent caught my attention in this entertainment district, though. Swimming through the crowd to get to this tent an obnoxious couple drunkenly bumps into me. Instead of any of us apologizing, the couple, who were definitely at fault, take steps towards me as if they are going to have the audacity to ask me what my problem is. Neither are dressed for Halloween so I do not have much in my mental arsenal to go on regarding that. The trashy young woman has a much meaner look on her face than the man. This feeling that begins to boil inside me is a mirror of what I felt the other night towards my now cleft-headed and handless former bully, that now rests in my Massachusetts forest, ugly and missing. I refuse to let the bitter impulse take over and ruin another night of joyful killing. Allowing my mind to wander for a few aggravated seconds I imagine both of these inebriated goons tied up on the floor in the Church of Elsewhere. Bound and gagged, laying down below the stage in front of the podium. I let them squirm and cry as I stand above them upon the stage and toss big heavy rocks with both hands up into the air to hopefully land on them. One hits his shin and cracks it. Another lands on her collarbone, also snapping something crucial. Maybe I miss a few, but it only makes their hysterics intensify when this happens. Eventually, they get hit in the head enough times for parts of their skulls to fracture and pierce their brains.

It is long before they excruciatingly bleed out or their bodies decide to quit. I soon give this fantasy no more attention and certainly do not act on the situation. Even if I were to throw a good killing night away on these oafs it would not be smart to engage or have any kind of altercation while this many people are around. Instead, I turn my attention back towards the velvet tent I was on course for.

-2-

Among the tents and stands that surrounded this one is some level of noise coming from each. Creatures of all kinds standing on their soapboxes to draw in the masses. All lively in their own way depending on what they were offering. This particular tent, however, had none of this pageantry. Just a closed elegant curtain and a thick soft black rope lightly tied at each end, with a beckoning sign for those who dared. As far as I can tell no one has accepted this dare like they have at all the others. The sign reads:

TURKISH FALCI
ACCEPT YOUR FATE, YE WHO DARE ENTER

Intrigued and still trying to come off the lingering annoyance of the drunk couple, it makes perfect sense to see what this is all about.

The knotted rope is untied and I back into the entrance flaps, being sure to tie it again before entering completely. The sign falls to the ground and I leave it. This reduces the chances of being disturbed by festival goers if things should take any kind of turn while inside that calls for solitude. It is smokey and reeks of incense. I can hardly see a thing but a soft glow that protrudes from another set of enclosing drapes. If there was anything to knock on to make my approach known I would have used it. I move forward confidently like I am supposed to be there, even without a proper announcement or invitation. When I lean in to open the fabric to the next room a graceful womanly voice entices me before my hand reaches up. This thick befitting accent, presumably Turkish, says "Come in, 'jeshoor eensun'. Come in."

I press through the drapes to a room lit by mosaicked Turkish lamps hanging from the walls and ceiling, with chains attached to tarnished brass fixtures. Glass of stained purple, orange, blue and brown filter the bulbs to radiate a somber moodiness to the room. Pillows of all sizes decorate the space as furniture. The massive rugs have patterns matching most of the pillows in the room, which I assume are Turkish motifs; squares and zigzags of fine detail that create larger squares and zigzags with the occasional figures that are geometrically floral in form. Every piece of these designs are a faded red or blue with varying shades of tan to fill any gaps in the pattern. An octagonal stone table sits low to the ground near the back of the room. It has a few of these pillows around it for sitting on. As I walk further into the room a woman swings open a curtain from a room unseen.

"Sit," she commands in an alluring cadence.

I take a seat at the table and ask her "What is all this? What does 'Fall-see' mean? From the sign out front."

"'Fahl-jeh'," she corrects my pronunciation. "It is a seer. One who divines things. Turkish language, 'jeshoor eensun'," she explains then realizes my blank stare means I have no idea what she just called me for the second time.

This Turkish woman begins writing something down on a piece of paper and I use the moment to take in as much as I can about her. She fits very well right into the atmosphere that has been cultivated in this smokey tent. Her hair is jet black. It comes through the lengthy mauve-purple headscarf she wears loosely. Her eyes almost seem purple themselves, but upon an honest perception they are an extremely dark hue of hazel. The well-fitting yet flowy dress she has on is nearly the same color and material as the tent, a velvety dark red with gold stitchings throughout.

She finishes writing and slides the note to me with a ring filled hand. It reads 'Cesur insan'.

"'Jeshoor eensun'. It means 'brave person'."

"I wouldn't call myself brave exactly. More unfearful than most, if that makes sense," I proclaim, amused.

"It does," she responds in a genuine manner and continues with her accent that halts and elongates at all the most mysteriously chosen places of her words.

"Through the dark and eerie umbras you trudge through, there is no icy hand to stroke your spine. And where most might churn out cold uneasy perspiration, you instead keep it within as unlikely nourishment."

This explanation feels like a poetic compliment; a way of saying I lack fear, but in a way that caters to the gimmick of her aggressively free-spirited atmosphere. As someone who is incapable of accepting a compliment, I respond by changing the subject.

"You sure like your incense."

"Bakhoor," she replies, while smelling the air. I take this to be the name of whatever fragrance that is currently lit. I do not care at all to follow up on this so, undaunted, I look around instead of experiencing the awkwardness I should probably feel. She allows the silence to linger, almost welcoming it as she lights another incense cone and places it in the dainty golden moon-shaped holder next to her. I almost forget that I am in the middle of a huge Halloween festival. The layer of curtain and tent material do a really good job of drowning out the noise from out there.

In the middle of this thought, the peculiar foreigner interrupts slowly with, "Okay now. I can perform tasseography and read tea leaves or, the traditional Turkish way for this kind of fortune telling, read coffee grounds. I can cast bones, osteomancy, and answer your questions about the future. Tarot divination. Crystal ball scrying. Palm, skull or aura reading. Oracle analysis through numerology, astrology or onomancy. The choice is yours if choice is what you choose. Otherwise, I can choose for you."

I am quietly thinking to myself about how this is simply a waste of time for me. This is charlatan business and I am only feeding into the scam. I should be out there enjoying myself the best way I know how. It also occurs to me that right now would be an opportune time to kill this fraudster. No one is around and probably no one has clocked me walking into the tent. I could grab and end her in the middle of the busy event without prying eyes to discover it. I get a rush from just considering it, but ultimately determine that the evening mischief is too early to start. But it would be just that easy.

I select the bone throwing, or osteomancy, from her options of divination as it was the most morbid. She retrieves a leather sack from a cabinet covered in gemstones behind her. I am handed the tan leather sack and told to focus on putting my energy into the items inside.

"Imagine all the elements of your life; worries, ambitions, romances, dreams, unanswered questions, work, creative endeavors, past, present and future. Take everything that does and could make you yourself and picture it as sand in your hands. Now envision that sand is thrown into the wind. And when it falls it is sucked up into the pouch you now hold in your hands. Take as long as you need."

I cannot explain why, but I uncharacteristically give in to this request and do exactly as she says. I do not believe in this sort of thing but am also curious to see the process, as well as the end result. Though, I do not have much faith it will lead to anything prophetic.

As I sit there and put my full intentions into this bag, the exotic woman keeps a one-sided dialogue going by telling me the contents inside of what is holding my attention.

"The curios held inside this hyena leather sack are a collection of bones and trinkets passed down to me from my nomadic ancestors. A leg bone from a caracal kitten and the clawed toe segment from its mother. The feathers and phalanx, this is the bone at the end of the wing, similar to a finger, of a mature ibis. A few vertebrae bones from the tail of an Anatolian leopard. A dozen whiskers from a Mediterranean seal. Five wolf teeth; two molars, two incisors and one canine. The beak of a squid. A smoky quartz gemstone of clouded coffee color. A rough agate gemstone of wavy orange, red, blue, yellow and white colors. One very old iron key that was hammered out by my great, great, great, grandfather. A rough wooden ring, made of Turkish walnut, that is almost just as old and that belonged to a woman killed on the evening of her 'nikah'; a small wedding ceremony. And the oldest item in the sack is a litra; a coin made of silver from Ancient Greece dating back over two-thousand years ago," she says solemnly, prideful of her wares.

"My kin, alive or spirited, still roam the Turkish countrysides and practice this divination with heirloom relics such as these and carry on the work of our ancestors."

I regain focus into the present moment from shifting my energy into the hyena leather. The woman seer takes notice of this and asks me to give the sack a few heartfelt shakes and cast the contents out into the circle. I had not noticed her do this, but she dumped out white sand on the stone table we sat at in the shape of a circle. This must have been done while I was focusing on the probable nonsense I was attempting. I toss all the contents of the bag onto the table. My eyes on the items that landed and hers looking deeply into mine. She then moves this stare down to the bones and her eyes widen.

"Both vertebrae pieces from the leopard's tail have landed outside the casting circle. I have never seen this before. This will certainly be an interesting reading," she says in a perplexed way while beginning to point at one of the teeth inside the sand ring.

"This here, the tip of the wolf's canine tooth touches the smoky quartz stone. And they are awfully close to the squid beak and caracal kitten bone. It appears as though the piercing ways about you are currently trying to draw themselves closer to a kind of stability. The smoky quartz represents the balancing of these ferocious objects and traits in a productive way. The proximity and meaning of the baby caracals leg bone could mean a sort of innocence in you or others. But, do you see how the leg is turned facing away? As if to indicate running away rather than towards. Truly peculiar."

She continued to fixate on the objects with focused eyes. Of course, I know this is all an act. No person in their right mind would believe this hokum. Regardless, I let the

Turkish seer act her heart out while I consider what I am going to do next. Do I kill her or allow her to live?

"Hmm, yes, so the agate stone and litra coin found themselves in the very middle of the circle. The significance of this, in relation to everything else going on here, is a tough one to figure out. The agate is a symbol of audacity and courage which also hints at clarity. The coin in the center might sometimes signify money as a central element to a person's reading. For our reading here I do not believe this to be accurate. It is more complex than money so far, so I do not think it is any kind of factor. It could, however, indicate a historical importance. Perhaps your history? Or perhaps the history you are making or going to make?" she says calmly and with a heavy accent.

I almost vocalize how right she is about the significant history I plan on making tonight. Instead, I keep my mouth shut and let her continue.

"The ibis wing bone and the rest of the wolf teeth are furthest from you. These are would-be crutches. They are still a part of your circle, but you have managed to push them far away. The seal whiskers are all evenly scattered around the circle and, as so, do not require much looking into; too uniform to read. The wooden wedding ring just barely touches the edge of the sand there. See? And the iron key is pointed directly at it. So, the ring itself, given the energy it has from where it came from, usually will represent some level of love or death or both. These meanings are not always the case, but it certainly feels like it in this one. The key that points to it means an opening up to love or death… or both. Or perhaps a barrier has already been broken regarding those things."

Her face dropped from a concentrated explanative earnestness to an uncomfortable seriousness, like she just realized something unbearable. Her once hearty voice turned to a cramped uneasy murmur as she went on in her still foreign way.

"Here is the most overwhelming part of your throw." She points with a trembling hand.

"Three ibis feathers forming a flawless triangle. The caracal mothers clawed toe bone right inside. The ibis feathers are a symbol of wrath as the ibis is a god in ancient cultures. With them forming this triangle, a weapon in our reading, representing a blade and point. It advances this as a symbol of wrath to something more severe as in a god-like or overly powerful sense of wrath. This is concerning. And to once again further the severity of power, the claw of the mother caracal is neatly inside. The claw here now represents another deadly piece of the 'you puzzle'. A sharp-minded, cunning hunter, she is. It is hard to say, but I hope there is a nurturer also hidden within this toe that is placed inside that potent feather triangle of unimaginable might."

She pauses for a second with a look on her face as if she wanted to cry. Then she regains some composure to present me with another thought that just struck.

"After seeing all of this, I believe the reason that the tail bones did not make it into the circle is because you lack balance in some form or another. The smoky quartz made it in because it is the allurer of balancing and unbalancing. I must say, you have managed to tantalize my percipience."

With that, she stands up and takes a step towards me. This gives me an overcoming feeling that I also need to stand up. I bump into the low standing table as I raise up to meet her stare. She takes one more step and leans into my face while grabbing the sides of my head with both of her ring-filled hands and kisses me deeply. Her eyes are closed and I stand frozen, except for my lips which are faintly kissing her lips back, without me telling them to. With my eyes open, staring into her closed ones, I feel this is the perfect moment to seize her by the hair and bash her head against that stone table. Maybe if I aim precisely and use enough of that wrathful force I can get some of those relics to jam themselves all the way into her skull as I am pounding her head into them.

I decide to control myself, in more ways than one. I give her a delicate shove backwards and turn to exit the tent. She does not say or do a thing as I walk my way to the exit. I stare at the exotic floor rug in this smokey, low lit room the whole way out.

I keep my focus as I step out of the tent, glad to have not given in and let that situation go any further than it did. I refuse to let it unnerve me as I set back out into the crowd of monsters.

-3-

The festival has amped up since I entered the Turkish soothsayers tent. With still a few hours away from the Harrowing Parade I realize that I am in the totally wrong location for my kind of fun, but in the right area. I need to get away from the big crowds. I begin this journey by getting myself away, through the festival grounds, and to the outskirts of them, where I start to stroll around aimlessly. On the edge of the festivities I can see across the street to different bars and restaurants all decked out in spooky decorations. There are houses around the next corner with dozens of children running in their costumes with pillow cases bulked up with candy as they cross streets to get to the next house, where they can beg for even more candy. Jack-o'-lanterns and haunting embellishments cover each and every house. Ghostly music and noises can be heard coming from many of these homes to set the mood for all the trick-or-treaters. I take one of these streets and follow it way down, past all the kids and noise and houses, until I am outside of the neighborhoods.

Following a backroad now, I find my wondering has led me to reach a cemetery. This cemetery is substantial in size and not very well lit. The clouded moon gives off just enough light to set the tone that someone like me would want while walking through a graveyard at night. White oak trees are strategically placed throughout the field of death with shrubs and bushes scattered about as well. My meandering has brought me through a thick of graves of all different sizes. Granite, marble and limestone headstones flood this public garden of deceased rest. Upright slabs with silly bible quotes etched into them surround and fill me with a yearning for mischief. Stone obelisks stand tall and demand attention to their host's resting place. Mausoleums of intricate detailing station themselves about as accommodation for those who could not care less or even realize where they are.

I struggle to comprehend why people spend so much money to create such a spectacle over another person's death. They lived and now they are gone; something that happens to everyone. Very few people have ever existed that deserve such a display and yet, nearly everyone gets some sort of ceremony and eternal resting spot designed just for them. Even many of the ones who are cremated are awarded some kind of headstone. I suppose people have always needed a physical location to unload their sentiments, especially when religion is involved; temples, shrines, graves, churches. I choose to use my Elsewhere Church for completely contradictory sentiments, though I recognize the irony in using it as a vessel at all for my own personal reprieve, just the same.

In the middle of my internal rambling I hear voices. Laughter, loud talking, heavy grunge music that currently saturates the airwaves and bottles clinking. I push through some small bushes to see a group of younger people who look to be not too far out of high school. They are lazily gathered in an area in front of a mausoleum. A thin and low to the ground metal bar wraps around this mausoleum area with a collection of tiny upright graves scattered within it, creating what can only be a family plot. A paltry little campfire burns as they sit on tombstones and ground or stand and drink whatever alcohol they have in their hand. One of the boys flicks a cigarette into the fire and takes a deep breath before looking like he has a statement to make. Before he can utter a single word he looks up and does a double take at me. I have been spotted in my obviously deficient surveillance place.

"Hey, dude!" the cigarette flicker yells in my direction.

"We can totally see you, man," another one says with a smirk on his face.

I reply while starting to walk in their direction, "Well, I guess I've gotten myself lost. Any chance you guys know where the Halloween festival is?"

"If you turn around and start walking the exact opposite direction as here you should pretty much end up at the town park," a blonde girl says before lighting a smoke.

"And what if I want to stay here with you?" I did not show it when I said this but I felt a very menacing urge inside.

"Listen, pal. We aren't really fucking interested in any-"
he almost finishes his dismissal of me before I interject.

"Do any of you like to trip?"

A girl with dark red hair perked up and gave her full
attention, "You have acid? Shrooms?"

The interest she showed in the acid I had caused all four
of the boys to then shift their attitude towards me into a more
welcoming one. These boys could not be more obvious in who
could pull their strings.

"Acid. Powerful stuff, too. Look," I say with confidence
as I pull twenty acid tabs from my wallet. I am now in the
random family gravesite plot, among them.

"Killer! What do you guys think about tripping tonight?
We already have a decent party started and all," the redhead
says to the group of four boys and the one other girl, who was
sitting close to her.

"How much per dose, pal?"

"Three dollars each. But I'll let a ten-strip go for
twenty-five."

"Done! It's on me everyone!" red hair then announces
to the group.

"I'm not sure I want to trip tonight. I have work early
tomorrow and my parents don't want me out late tonight
anyway. They'll throw a fucking fit if I walk in when the sun is
coming up again," the blonde girl with many face piercings
says.

"I'm with Wilda. Not a great night to trip," a jockish
boy eagerly says as if he is going to be rewarded for his loyalty.

"I'll bet you are. You two are just a couple of sticks in
the mud, always. Even when I offer to pay for everybody. And
all of us rode our bikes here so it's not like we're gonna get
pulled over or anything. We are all twenty years old, or just

about to be the big two-oh, and neither of you ever learned how to have any real fun."

"Oh whatever, Pippa. That's hardly the truth. I will still stay and drink until you guys start feeling that acid. Then Myles is gonna walk me home. Right, Myles?" Wilda says to the red-haired girl, who I now know is Pippa, and Myles, the jock boy who is also declining the LSD.

"Yeah, that sounds good to me," replied Myles.

"Okay whatever, let's just drop already," one of the still unnamed boys says.

I hand over ten tabs of the acid to Pippa, who is sitting down on a small headstone in front of the little fire. She rummages around in her purse and pulls out a crisp twenty dollar bill with five crumpled one dollar bills.

Pippa and three of the boys pop a tab into each of their mouths almost immediately after the transaction. The other two, Wilda and Myles, stand firm in their decision not to indulge.

"Enjoy your evening, everyone. I should take my leave. Still have to find the town Halloween festival, you know," I say, but not really meaning it.

"No way, man. At least stay and have a beer with us. Shot of rum?"

I decline the offer and walk back out into the brisk night toward the unoccupied parts of the cemetery maze. I do this slowly, though, so I can observe. I wait for them to stop paying attention to me and start once again on each other. When I am sure they have omitted me from their awareness I casually pick up one of their bicycles and dash to my truck on it. I open up the door and retrieve the backpack that I prepared earlier. Lock up and race back to the cemetery to sneak the borrowed bike back to where I had taken it from. Easy. Now, I sit, wait and watch the group of young friends carry on with their celebration.

They cheers their beers and pass the bottle of rum around. Cigarettes are smoked continuously by all of them, except for when a joint is lit. It is a shame that I could not find a place out of their view that is just a little bit closer. I am finding it hard to hear most of what they are saying, but at the very least I can study them visually. All of them are dressed mostly in black. One of the girls has on platform boots and the other has sneakers. Black stockings and black jeans. Band t-shirts with dark colored jackets to cover their arms. Both decorated with jewelry on their hands, around their necks and on their ears. Blonde Wilda has a few looped rings on one side of her nose and one through the center of her bottom lip. Also, on her eyebrow and many going up the length of her ears, much more than Pippa. They both stay comfortably seated while the four boys pal around by shoving each other and put one another in the occasional headlock. They are all dressed more or less the same. Blue jeans and black or dark shirts. Two of them with loose flannels over the shirts. Myles, with a black jean jacket and the last one with a black leather jacket.

-4-

I have been here watching from the shadowy concealing bushes for roughly twenty-five minutes when, finally, a giggling Pippa stands up and her legs wobble like noodles as she tries to walk. This is not drunk walking. She is high on the acid now. This adds up as it has been close to an hour since they took the stuff. She walks a few more steps and calls it quits by taking a seat on a different gravestone. In their carefree frolicking I cannot help but wonder if any of them has experienced real anguish or shock in their lives. To my perception, it feels like they had been born into this town where their sensibilities were never truly tested or challenged.

Wilda gets up and seems to be giving her departing farewells. As she starts to walk away from the group she motions to a reluctant Myles, who appears to want to stay. I really wish I could make out what they were saying as this is becoming more and more entertaining to me. Myles has now given in and walks away with her.

Pippa yells out to them in a crystal clear voice, "Whiny Wilda wins again!"

This is surely meant to reference how she conquered Myles and his apparent disposition of not wanting to leave. Both Myles and Wilda leave with peeved looks on their faces. The remaining four have quite the opposite looks fixed to their faces. Full of euphoria and wonder.

Crouched down in the bushes, almost directly in the walking path of Wilda and Myles as they leave the gathering, I wait attentively. They stroll past me, without noticing a thing, and I follow behind, leaving enough space between them and me to not interrupt their mission home. I hide behind the occasional gravestone or tree as we approach the edge of the cemetery and start of a woodsy trail.

My backpack is dropped and hidden by a polished obelisk gravestone before entering the woods in slow pursuit of the two locals, being sure to grab the hammer and knife out of the bag to take with me. We enter the woods and I ditch my socks and boots. The crunching of dead leaves under my footwear is too detectable. Bare feet will aid in keeping delicate steps while quieting my movement.

I already feel a positive flow in how I am managing this night. My terrifying dream counselors were really on to something. This is how these doings of mine should feel; guided by psychic pleasure of pure drive, not propelled by an agitated frustration through anger. The unwanted impulse does not exist in this moment. I have tamed it all night, in instances when I could have let loose and released the fiend that would, for sure, eventually cause disappointment in myself. This newer fiend, that I now see myself able to become, is within my clutches; feeling more like my own captain now. I am doing my best to hold on to him, onto me. I think of Eeka and am grateful for her coming into my life, or rather, me forcing myself into hers. Without our experience together I may have never begun this inner renaissance. Eeka's slain body falls from my thoughts as I find myself sprinting.

With a swift stride I quickly gain an approach on my prey, relying mostly on my big toes and ball underneath them at the front of my feet to carry me quietly up to Myles. I crack him in the top of the head with my hammer before he even hears me coming. The night is quiet still. I expected a scream from Wilda but I got nothing but silent horrific countenance. Myles was not quite out cold. He moved a bit trying to get composure but the hammer's knock to the head was mighty, so he would surely need more time. Wilda and I stand face to face a few paces apart. The trees rustle what is left of their dying leaves with the help of the breeze. Moonbeams fall all around us during our standoff in the woods. My hammer has fallen in the excitement, but the knife is firmly bonded to my hand.

Frozen in time from terror, this is how Wilda appears. I can almost notice her quaking to some degree, but it is possible that this is my imagination. I take the initiative to advance while she is still in her petrified state. I move toward her slowly, trying not to startle her into running away or fighting me, as if she were a scared dog that I was trying to pet. Her wide-eyed stare was looking at, or possibly through me as I kept an unhurried focus by counting the piercings on her face. By the time I got to nine I was close enough. She still stood unable to move, with that frightful look, even as I put one hand on her shoulder and plunge my knife into her stomach. She begins to gurgle a scream when I move the blade in all directions around inside her stomach. The squirming turned into pulling away, but my hand that graced her shoulder now moved around the back of her neck and landed on her other shoulder so I could pull her close in what might look like an affectionate hug. My arm had her head locked, with our chins on each other's shoulders and the sides of our faces pressing against one another. Her drunken and shocked resistance was no match for my dynamic hold on her. The knife continued to wiggle around in her belly while we danced in the woodland moonlight. Soon the hole was big enough to fit my whole fist into, never letting go of the knife as I pushed in. The insides were warm and slimy. I did my best to push my arm in as far as possible, which was nearly up to the elbow. I moved eagerly through organs that fought against me. When this happened I twisted the knife around to make some room. I did not want this embrace to end, but Wilda began to go limp and the deadweight of her body was giving me the closure I needed in order to end our intimate moment. I loosened the lock my arm had around her head so I could pull her back from me a bit before I ripped my limb out from her torso. Her eyes danced in different directions as I did this and she began to gurgle out blood. The grip I had on her shoulder and the way I was propping her up through the stomach hole was released. She dropped to the leafy October ground.

I start to think about how I am going to get the viscera bits and blood cleaned off of my naked arm, but am also thankful I had the foresight to take my coat off before this. Just then, as I consider the gore stuck to me while looking down at the masterpiece I have made, I was struck with a rock to the back of my head. Myles had come to and with vengeance. His blow to my head was not nearly as powerful as mine was to his. Still, I dropped hard to the ground. Myles stood above me with an unsteady balance. He was still impaired from the hammer and the alcohol and the weed. I could see a streak of blood down the side of his neck coming from his head. Tears were welling up in his eyes while he looked back and forth from his friend's lifeless gored corpse and me on the ground staring up at him. As I looked at him I could sense he was not the type to kill, even pushed to limits such as these. Of course, there was no way for me to be sure, but I turned to the side in order to push myself up with my hands. I was going to make a move to get up and fight this trembling opponent, but he was able to land a forceful kick directly to my stomach. This blew out all the air from inside of me and I landed face down gasping for breath. The rock he now had was brought down hard to the center of my back. There is not much I can achieve now. My arms reached out to the sides and gripped dirt and leaves. It was all I could do, besides consider if this guy was going to kill me or have me hauled off to prison.

The tree in front of my straining face has knots in the bark. A cluster of four of these knots sort of resembled Ghost's face. Three oval shapes; eyes and mouth. And a triangle for the nose. This makes me think of the journey that brought me here and everything I am about to lose. Maybe this is the 'life flashing before your eyes' thing they say happens before you die. I found my dream home and I have hobbies that give me unbounded contentment now. All the while, I have embarked on this recent spiritual journey to becoming a better, more refined me. Now, it is all about to go away.

How could I let this happen, at the pinnacle of this life change, with Ghost staring right at me. Judging me. Encouraging me?

I am unable to see Myles, but there is no doubt he still stands over me, getting ready for another blow with the rock. In front of me, and right below the Ghost tree, is a broken branch the length and thickness of my arm. With my bloody hand I snatch the offering that Ghost has presented and hurl a palmful of dirt with the other hand into the face of my adversary. Myles steps back once and spits while wiping his eyes with his sleeve. I, still winded from the kick to my stomach, instantly pull myself together as best I can and swing the hardy stick into the temporarily blinded boy's temple. He throws his rock, tryingly in my direction, before he topples over. The rock hits me in the shoulder and my weapon goes down. The foe is staggering back to his feet. I see the hammer that laid him out originally and find it most opportune to wield it once more to finish the job it started. A sloppy rush and grasp of the leafy hammer gives me the upper hand once again. I charge Myles and land the hammer right between his eyes, assuredly breaking the bridge of his nose and forehead, among probable other things. He is down. On his back with all limbs spread out wide. I do not waste any time and sit on his belly while hammering his face in. Beat after beat to his forehead, his nose, both eyes, and mostly his mouth. I smash out all of his front teeth and continue whaling down to try and get all the back ones. His jaw is in pieces at this point and hard to tell if it is even still attached. There is just too much blood and gore to make any definitive presumptions. His eyes, popped. Sockets, cracked and mangled. Nose, nonexistent as I have made my way to working the hammer into this region of the face. If there is a nose left it is deep within his skull now.

What I see is not a human head anymore. It looks more like a heavily sauced bowl of pasta with ears. I almost feel a sense of pride in being able to frenzy-hit him this many times and with such stamina, all while still being so short of breath. The invigorating rush I felt once I had the upper hand with that first crack is indescribable, but it is surely what carried me into having the ability to do this to his face. I get myself up off of him and jump on his chest as if I was trying to break through ice. His chest collapses under me. Just when I think I am done with him I lean down and give his face one more good sideswipe with the hammer, sending bits of bone and teeth and meat over to Ghost.

A checkup on Wilda shows me she is still dead. I suspected this. But something still needs to be done with her. Her corpse pales in comparison to what I have done with Myles. Since there is already a welcoming pit slashed into her stomach it is obvious that this is where I will start. Wilda's belly opening is penetrated a few times more in order to pull out lengths of both large and small intestine. These are conveniently located just inside the knife hole. I have to reach up further to pull out a piece of liver that must have been cut off earlier while my blade did its exploring. The full spleen came out as well, along with a handful of tender pancreas. I left the severed extracted parts laying down next to her. The intestines were still connected inside, but what I pulled out of them from her rested all over as it erupted outward from her stomach.

I leave the gruesome scene in the woods to go check on the others, that is, after the final task of procuring the forty-three dollars from their wallet and purse.

-5-

I walk up confident that the others are tripping hard by now. They have no idea that I had actually been watching them and then went on to slay their friends since after they last saw me.

"Hey everyone," I say, waving with the arm and hand that are doused in drying blood.

All four of them appear anxious at the intruder approaching their party. This is understandable given that they are peaking on LSD right now. Any change in atmosphere during this will heighten internal alarm bells for a moment. Two of the boys catch themselves and toughen up as fast as they can. Those two start to leave the gravesite plot that they have been stationed in since I have known them. This quickly turns into the realization that it is only me. Their drug dealer and new friend.

"Hey, man!" one of the boys says welcomingly.

"You scared the shit out of us."

"Sorry about that, fellas. And lady. I came back to check up on you."

"Shit, man, these tabs are pretty damn strong."

"Should I have warned you?" I say, knowing full well I already mentioned their potency.

"No way! We're having a blast! It's been long laughs and then a bunch of quiet reflections or whatever. We don't get acid this strong around here."

All of their pupils were black, dilated beyond belief from the drug.

"Great. The festival was kind of a drag, so I took a tab myself not too long ago. Then I came to trip with you guys. Is that okay with you?" I lie to gain more of their trust.

"Hell yeah, it's okay with us. Should've just stayed. This acid feels amazing," Pippa calmly mutters while laying in the grass with her eyes closed.

The three boys all relax back to how they were before I strolled up. The one they call Jord nearly falls over off the memorial stone that he starts to take a seat on. This is good solidifying evidence to how gone they are on the acid, as I expected. I interrupt the quiet mellow vibe that begins to take over.

"Do you guys mind if I just sit here quietly and get lost in my thoughts? I'm so messed up on this stuff. Definitely peaking."

A few seconds of silence occurs. I said all that because I know that this is where they are in their trip. The settling down and buckling up for another introspective spell of an acid peak.

"No worries, man," is all I get between the four of them.

They are laying back and completely lost in the trip. Totally vulnerable. No one could have planned this better.

Everyone is down now with shut eyes and untold visuals going on inside their minds. I watch each of them and try to devise a plan. They all might as well be asleep, except for Jord, who fishes up his joint then tosses it. Now, they go from looking like they were sleeping to looking comatose.

There has to be quite a bit of nuance in handling a situation like this. I cannot start on one without ruffling the rest of them. It is four against one when it comes down to it, regardless of how inebriated they are. I not only need to worry about being overpowered, but also if one gets away and squeals then it turns into one against the world. I should not forget that I am also semi-injured and must remember that there is no walking away at this point. If I were to turn around and walk away now then eventually the two mutilated bodies that I left in the woods would be found. An investigation would be done and these four survivors would connect all necessary dots for the investigators. All of these pieces to the current high stakes puzzle I have begun must fit together perfectly and in the proper order. Anything less and I can lose everything. But it is true that everyone needs to dance with the devil sometimes, especially me. And I enjoy having to calculate complex situations to finish the dance.

Their eyelids flutter as if they are dreaming in a heavy sleep. Hands occasionally move around at their sides to feel the sensation of the cool grass they lay in. The campfire remains small and flashing. I lean against the mausoleum to plot, while watching the moon bathe them within their contained ecstasy. Peaceful on the outside and euphorically chaotic inside. All while set to the aura of Halloween night.

I approach the closest lying down boy, who I presume is named Nolan judging by one of the patches sewn to his leather jacket. All in one motion I rip the mesh trucker hat from his head before bringing a hammer ruthlessly down at the top of his forehead, returning the hat to cover the wound. Nolan is dead. I make sure of this by poking and strangling him without any movement on his part. With any reasoning on anyone's part, he looks asleep or lost in his hallucination with no excuse to be disturbed. The hat conceals his death dent so perfectly that no one should notice unless they removed it or paid extremely close attention to detail. Which they will not do while tripping. Quick and to the point without any hiccups. This was less amusing than I would like it to have been with him, but it had to be done. There are playful risks we take in life and then there are stupid ones. With him out of the way the odds have shifted moreover in my favor of being outnumbered by three to one now.

Jord pipes up, "Hey guys, do you remember last Halloween when we came here? And Myles told us that creepy ghost story his father told him, from like a really long time ago about Cornham?"

"Yeah, totally! He said it all was true. Olly, you almost pissed your pants from it," Pippa announces to us, giving a name to the last unnamed boy here.

"First of all, I did piss my pants. Second, it was because I was too wasted to know up from down. Pretty sure I fully pickled my liver last year."

Everyone alive begins to open their eyes. The vibe has shifted towards talking and away from introspection. Nolan stays quiet, deep in thought, as far as anyone is concerned.

"Is everyone else still getting crazy visuals? These gravestones are fucking mesmerizing. I swear they are breathing," says the blue-eyed and slicked back brown-haired Olly.

"I am."

"Definitely."

"Oh yeah, I can't turn it off," I had to chime in to continue the lie that I am hallucinating with them.

"Hey brother, what's with all the red? Looks like you're painted up to go to a football game or something," Jord examined me.

"It's supposed to be blood. Some folks at the festival didn't think I was dressed up enough for Halloween, so they did this. Corn syrup and red dye I think."

I am enjoying the suspense in not knowing how this will turn out. At the same time, I am beginning to wonder when the clock will start ticking for when the drugs begin to taper off and the pleasant suspense slides to sour over-postponement. This starts to turn my guts inside out, like Wilda's; hypothetically of course. I also start to wonder if I should have actually taken a bit of LSD. I did so on Eeka's night and that whole experience was the catalyst for my recent positive activation.

"Can I show you guys something?" I say earnestly, like I have something they really need to see.

"Lay it on us. Just please, no more drugs," Olly says, chuckling softly.

I glance over at each of them to make sure they are still in the state I believe them to be in. Of course, they are. Eyes still looking like black olives that occasionally flutter and float, due to the visual effects caused by the acid.

"Okay, great!" I reply, reaching for my bag.

I stand up and walk behind Jord, who is sitting up like the rest of them. I drop my backpack and pull out a short roll of barbed razor wire from it. I carefully uncoil a length of it, after putting a pair of work gloves on, and madly put it over Jord's head and around his neck. I pull it tight, but not quite tight enough to pierce any skin, I think. Now, I stand us both up from behind him by pulling up on the wire coated with small double-sided razor blades. I can sense all three of their confusion now, especially Pippa and Olly since I can see their faces. They can also see my face and I know that the crazed look I wear now is way out of character from anything they have seen from me yet. Pippa and Olly stay seated while I hold Jord firm and close to me with the razor wire. I can tell they want to stand.

"Stay sitting!" I command in a very unhinged way.

I have to appear as unstable as possible. If they have any doubt that I am capable of killing their friend then they may charge at me or take off running. I need to have total control of the situation.

"Now just listen. Jord here is going to die if you don't do exactly what I say," I have perfected the maniacal voice and pitch.

"Please don't! We will do-" Pippa begins.

"Shut up! Just listen," I once again command while shaking Jord by his razor-wrapped neck.

They both purse their mouths tight. Eyes still black and floaty.

"Take these handcuffs, Olly."

I very quickly reach at the pair of handcuffs tucked in my pants and throw them sloppily towards the two anxious friends. My hand rightly returns to its place holding one end of the razor wire. This speedy gesture was done with the confidence that Jord is too intoxicated to try and escape before he knew what was happening.

"Good. Now I want you to cuff your left wrist to Pippa's right ankle. Make sure you lock it tight. And you will probably want to stay sitting down for this."

Olly's glazed over and tear-filled eyes give a hard squeezing blink and a tear rolls down from one side. He is choking back all kinds of fear-driven emotions. But, he does exactly as I say.

"Great, Olly. Again, make sure it's tight. If I go over there and they aren't tight I am going to kill your friend."

Olly double-checks them and I hear a couple more faint clicks from the handcuffs.

"That was a close one, right Jord? How are you doing by the way?"

"Fuck you, man!"

I can see some light bleeding from his neck. Most likely from when I shook him. Nolan remains dead silent. The others have noticed this by now but have been given fair warning not to speak, just to listen.

"Now, I only want your money. I did the same thing with Wilda and Myles and made forty-three dollars from them. My plan is to take your money and everything will be cool. You will be able to see your friends soon if everything goes my way. Olly, do you have something to say?"

Olly speaks up nervously, "Here. Here's my wallet."

"Olly, I get the impression you've never been around anything truly traumatic. Never had a friend or family member pass away yet. Never even been in trouble. You're dealing with this like a dog being disciplined for the first time. Confused and scared to a further degree than someone who has had these essential life experiences. Am I close?"

"Yes," he says shakily.

I immediately pull the razor wire as tight as I can, pressing it into his friend Jord and grinding it against his throat with all of my strength. I do this while holding intense deranged eye contact with Olly. Jord resists and wiggles and turns around to face me so he can grab my arms and fight back. In his turning motion, he had made things worse by further butchering himself with all the hungry razors. He is high and drunk and severely injured which makes him no match for me. I break loose of his grip on my arms without having to let go of the razored necktie. Hopping back behind him, I hold him much tighter while his arms go all different directions before weakening. Lowering his body to the ground while Olly and Pippa continue to make their horrified noises. During the whole altercation I rarely ever lost eye contact with Olly.

Tonight, I have given Olly a lifetime of emotions to deal with all at once. If I were to let him live out the rest of his life he would most definitely develop all sorts of mental problems from this experience. He would be dealing and working through them as long as he lived. He would never be bored again. This gift is too great to give to someone like him.

These remaining two are struggling and trying their hardest to get up and run away, but the awkward way they are tethered to each other makes any kind of effective escape impossible. They are also not in the right state of mind to work together or have any kind of semi-constructive chance. Olly stands up and tries to run in one direction while Pippa, with her disheveled red hair, tries to crawl in another. They tire themselves out before long.

"Enough. Just sit there and please pay attention. Or don't, I actually don't really care. None of this is for you, so do what you will."

They let go of trying to escape. Even if they did work together they would never be fast enough for me not to catch them. If they decided to rush me I would simply overpower them. Their shortcomings at the moment are too numerous and being shackled hand and foot to each other would equal absolute failure against me. So they lay back down on the grass and try to at least overcome their high condition to make sense of everything. A difficult, but more suited adversary for them. They steal glances away from me and fix them on Nolan. It is unspoken, but they know he is deceased. While they lay there and catch their breath with full attention back on me, I crouch down to a probably dead Jord and take hold of the razor wire that is embedded in his neck once again. I make a few wraps around my gloved hands with it so there is optimal grip and control. The heavy sawing with the bladed wire that I begin doing clearly unsettles Pippa and Olly. Pippa shrieks while Olly gags and vomits. They are both crying while they react in their own ways until finally Jord goes completely limp at his neck. I have sawed through all of the neck flesh. I let Jord lay face down while I part the two sides of his neck meat where I cut through. This is to expose the axis vertebrae of his spine to a greater extent. When the flesh is parted enough and out of the way, I begin to bash the exposed spine bone until it is shattered. A fairly easy task compared to the other things I have done tonight. It finally shatters and his head is free from the body that carried it.

Olly and Pippa look worse than ever; still exceptionally high and probably still very drunk as I go through Jord's wallet and help myself to the five spot and few dollar bills. Their appearance worsens further when I pick up their dear friend Jord's severed head by its hair and gently place it in my backpack.

-6-

Another two sets of handcuffs are presented to the horror-stricken victims. One set goes on Pippa's wrists, securing her hands together in front of her. The other set gets Olly's right hand fastened to Pippa's left ankle. The idea here is to have it so me and Olly are carrying Pippa. He gets her legs, each hand holding the ankle it is cuffed to, and I hold her arms. The system works flawlessly as we carry her to the edge of the woods, holding her like double dutch jump ropes.

We stop so everyone can catch their breath and Olly can vomit once more. I ponder if they know I am going to kill them or if they are deluded enough to think there is a chance they can be let go. The mind and body will always strive for survival even in hopeless situations. Even after seeing their friend brutally decapitated by a madman stranger that they were stupid enough to trust, something tells me they still have hope to make it out of here alive if they abide by my orders and stay model prisoners. I can only hope that they keep this level of despairing obedience or it will be a troublesome ride back to the Elsewhere Church for all of us.

Olly and I lift Pippa back up and breach into the woods. Pippa looks more uncomfortable and sags further down with every few steps we take. Regardless of his distraught state, Olly powers through it to get the job I have assigned to him done and he does it without protest. For this, I am grateful. It is like going out hunting for deer, but instead of shooting the beast and dragging him back, he instead agrees to follow you to your vehicle to be shot.

The apathetic blankness that cloaks him suddenly turns back to dread when we approach the lurid bodies of his two friends, Wilda and Myles. Olly lets go of Pippa's legs when he makes horrific sense of what he sees. When this happens Pippa's legs fall down and take Olly's tethered arms down with them, causing his whole self to come crashing over in a defeated topple. I simply drop the upper half of Pippa, who now sees what Olly sees. A facially unrecognizable Myles and a recognizably gutted Wilda. Her darkened bloody intestines spilling out from her stomach and strewn around her body is one of the most visually pleasing things I have ever seen. This is the kind of image I would have professionally painted and hung on my wall. The experience happening now must be so surreal for them. This is a great moment.

Tears and wails come from each of the awkwardly shackled pair that likely never thought this night would turn out the way it is. Four friends dead, in untimely and unnatural ways, because they decided to trust an unfamiliar face.

"I should probably come clean about something. This isn't corn syrup on my arm."

Their sobs continue through my confession. I would like to hurry this up and can obviously force them to, but I stop myself a little bit longer. Gather ye rosebuds, as well as smell the roses and all the sentiments along those lines, I suppose. I breathe a deep meditative breath, feeling satiated with how the night has gone so far for me. No true anxiousness or vexation has presented itself at all. I am purely able to just enjoy it.

I nearly forgot how far away my truck was parked. There is no chance that I could get away with embarking all the way to it with these two. It is best that they stay here, I figured. While they fall deeper into tearful hopelessness I open my backpack and gingerly remove Jord's amputated head. This is so I can get to the glass ether inhaler I have wrapped in a towel. My only option is to leave them here while I go retrieve my truck to park it closer. A minor oversight in an otherwise fruitfully efficient series of plots. The tedious task of getting to the truck in a timely fashion will require me to first backtrack to the cemetery plot and reclaim a bicycle. After that, I can dash to my trusty automobile. To ensure my captives do not get away or yell for help I have to knock them out. Force will not be

necessarily while I have ether. My fourth and last set of
handcuffs are snapped on to Olly's left ankle and the other side
is to an ankle of the faceless Myles.

"What are you doing with us?" queried Pippa, with
eyeliner running down her cheeks.

"Right now I am making sure you can't go anywhere or
yell out to anyone," I say standing over the two living victims,
freshly tethered to a dead one.

Olly is shaking uncontrollably from fear. He is now
broken. There is almost no resistance or jumpiness when I slip
the strapped mouthpiece of the ether inhaler over his head. He
then slips into unconsciousness.

"Now for-" I begin saying while turning to Pippa, but
she has leaned forward and starts sinking her teeth into my leg.

I shake my leg and grab ahold of her hair. She holds her
bite strong while being thrown around in her cuffed sitting
position. I am very careful not to kick the glass ether container
during this bout. I move my clenched fist from her hair and put
it on the back of her neck to squeeze her pressure points. She
fights the pain at first but then concedes. My leg feels like it is
on fire but still plenty usable for a good kick to Pippa's
stomach. While she is out of breath I dump some ether on a
hand towel and hold it over her mouth for a few seconds. She is
out. I soak the same hand towel and throw it in a plastic bag.
The opening of the bag is then made to fit over her nose and
mouth. I use electrical tape to secure the bag to her face by
wrapping a generous amount of it around her head. This is a
makeshift ether inhaler that I am positive will work for the time
I need it to.

I give one last look at the glorious snaking entrails
coming out of Wilda before sprinting back to the mausoleum
area where the bicycles are. Jord's headless corpse lays there

next to Nolan's peaceful body. In college, a professor once speculated to us that it is possible the brain has activity for a short while after decapitation. If this turns out to be true, I wonder if the awareness is present on a cognitive level. It is a fascinating thought to think, after I sawed his neck and bashed out his connecting vertebrae, that he might in some way have the final ability to hear his best friends scream in horror. A Halloween miracle, to me at least, if it is true.

I remember to clean their wallets of any cash inside before continuing on with the mission.

Pedaling as fast as I possibly can to make it to my truck, I pass the woods where I left the unconscious prisoners. Pass through the streets I have navigated a few times before. Pass the thinning mass of trick-or-treaters and arrive at my truck just a handful of blocks away from the festival. The bike is ditched and traded for my inconspicuous blueish grey pickup truck. All the appropriate laws of the road are obeyed while I am making my way back to the cemetery woods to pick up my shipment. This takes longer than riding the bike because I have to stop and creep around all the costumed candy beggars.

I park the truck off the road right up against the woods where the cargo unconsciously waits to be hauled away. Everyone is exactly how they were left. First, I remove the two ankle-to-foot pairs of cuffs and lock one of those sets to only Pippa's ankles. Then I put the other set to Olly's ankles. Next, I remove the handcuffs from Myles and Olly's ankle and fasten Olly's wrists together with them. Now both prisoners are bound by wrist and ankle separately. I drag Olly to the back of my truck and pull him up inside of it.

This brings to mind Eeka and when I had to do this very thing with her.

I enter the woods again and recover Pippa. She is noticeably much lighter to drag, so I almost feel I should be carrying her instead, but stick with the dragging; no need to show off as chivalry is dead for the moment. I begin to pull her up into the truck without any problems when all of a sudden a spotlight blinds me. I drop Pippa's limp body from the tailgate where I was lifting her and cover my eyes with my flanneled arm. I am too focused on the blinding to be nervous. When I lower my arm the spotlight is gone. It has been replaced with flashing red and blue police car lights.

"Stop what you are doing and get down from the tailgate," an authoritative voice says through a speaker in the police car.

I do as he says and hop down. The flashing red and blue lights on top of the car are then switched off. The spotlight, however, is back on and shining right on me and everything around me. I remain calm. I reminisce and repeat a mantra to myself.

Do not panic. Everything is how it should be. Just go with it.

The officer approaches and asks, "What the hell have you got going on here? No sudden movements, okay?"

"Yes, officer. I think she is unconscious now from the drop. But she was incredibly drunk which is why I was helping her up in there," I say confidently to the stout police officer.

He runs his index finger and thumb down the sides of his handlebar mustache while looking around my business, trying to make sense of it.

"Why in the truck bed? Why not in the front or the cab?"

"We have three children and I don't want them seeing their mother like this."

He takes out his flashlight and walks towards the front of the truck to inspect. He makes his slow cautious approach to the side door and passes me all together while still trying to ask questions.

"Explain to me what you folks were doing all the way over-"

A clunk to the head with a wrench and three rapid stabs through the back of the neck with a knife before he even hits the ground. How thankful I am and baffled that he, a police officer, would turn his back on me at a scene like this one. No backup with him or anything. This might be my most satisfying achievement yet tonight. To think, I was as close as I could ever be to being arrested or shot dead. No more exploits of devious nature. No more freedom at all. The final curtain was about to fall. Closing credits nearly started scrolling. The other shoe threatened to drop harder than I dropped Pippa just now. But no, the fool in uniform let his guard down and actually turned his back to me. This intrusion was not welcomed one bit, but the bliss that followed my initial mental discomposure from the thought of getting caught is pleasantly undefinable. Almost any unplanned killing that I am forced into without choice, like the rude man from yesterday, will be lamentable from now on. I have no desire to participate in these kinds of artlessly impulsive assaults. But this one feels different in a way that I cannot put my finger on. It could be because my freedom was threatened and I resolved this threat. It could be because this will be such a high-profile death; he is a cop, after all. It could also be that I am overcome with the holiday spirit because of what I have done tonight and what is still yet to come. Seeing this cop on the ground in front of me almost starts to make me feel invincible, but I shake this delusion off quickly before it seeds itself too deep. The truth is, I will treasure this instance forever. I took control of securing my own future by not letting the police officer take control of it himself. It is a shame that I have to rush out of the moment, but I have my doubts about being this fortunate when the next bit of trouble rolls up.

The cop is not dead, though. My truest preference is to set him on fire, but this would make a huge counterintuitive scene. Instead, I stomp on his head a bit. I did not hear any cracks but this shoeing will surely cause some hemorrhaging. For good measure I stab at his head a few adequate times. It seems like everything is reminding me of Eeka tonight. No time to dissect this train of thought. Pippa gets thrown in the back with Olly and both are strapped back up to the ether. I probably was not too far away from having to deal with at least one of them regaining consciousness.

I pass through the neighborhoods at a neatly slow pace like an upstanding member of society would. It is late and almost no one seems to be out. Decorations remain lit and vibrant. Jack-o'-lanterns still house flamed candles. At this moment I decide I want to purchase pumpkins to bring back to Elsewhere. It is the perfect opportunity since I can no longer find them around the Saint Ox area and I am not worried about the two in the back. Even without the ether they have had enough substances and excitement to warrant unconsciousness. Now that everything has appeared to calm down in the streets, I can casually go back to the festival at the park and pick up some of those fresh pumpkins I saw earlier. A better idea would be to just take them off of a porch but there is no sense in blowing my cover now, after everything that has happened tonight.

My lapse in remembering the Harrowing Parade has
turned my plans upside down some. Streets are sectioned off
from cars by blockades on every possible and practical way to
the festival grounds. Since I have it in my head to get a few
pumpkins to liven up the church again, I am not letting this
setback deter me. I park a few blocks further than my previous
spot and start walking. I cannot believe how late it has gotten.
Already a bit past midnight, so the parade has started and I
expect it to be hectic. There is no way to get to where I need to
be without encountering a fair share of the Harrowing Parade.

-7-

The parade is utterly overwhelming. This wild spectacle far
exceeds my expectation of what a town Halloween parade
would be. I suppose this is why it is held at this late witching
hour.

The parade procession itself is quite intensely feverish.
Fire spitters on stilts set the mood ablaze with constant fireballs
aimed in every direction coming from their crazed painted
faces. Demented clowns run from the center of the cobblestone
street out to the crowds of people and laugh hysterically or
shriek unintelligible words. Twisted contortionists with tight
ragged clothing bend and flip down the parade path with
gigantic smiles stuck on their expressions. Candy and mini
festive alcohol containers are thrown out nonstop. Demons ride
on unholy floats spitting blood-like liquid. Ghosts with white
see-through sheets, so you can just barely make out the naked
female form underneath, walk alongside them. Werewolves bite

the heads off of baby dolls with their long gnashing teeth. Old-
timey carnival music is pumped through speakers that can
hardly be heard over the racket of the attendees.

I wind and weave my way through the crowd of
creatures and sensual costumes. Rows of people line the wide
sidewalks and storefronts with eyes fixed on the freak show that
passes them by in the street. Mixed throughout the spectators
are groups forming small parties. They play drinking games,
they sing, they kiss, they wrestle and disorderly ramble on with
one another. A muscled up vampire runs down the sidewalk
with his topless maiden on his shoulders. The bare chested girl
swings her shirt around above her head while she merrily
screams intoxicated nonsense the whole way. I pass folding
tables along these parade sidelines selling skull jewelry and
Halloween masks with an unspoken and illegal option to
purchase a beer or some weed. I care about nothing but getting
to the park where the festival pumpkin stands might still have
that merchandise I am risking everything to purchase. It will be
a long time before having the option to buy pumpkins again, so
I will put up with this hectic navigation to get to the ripe
Halloween treat I crave to have gracing my church home. There
are more alcoholic drinks and fake blood spilled on me than I
care to dwell on. Dressed-up people rudely bumping into me as
they push through the mass of festival goers and me rudely
bumping back into them.

I claw my way through to a break in the fleshy horde
that leads to the street. I am now front and center to view the
parade. Caring very little about what is happening on the
pavement I instead wait for the perfect moment to dart across
the marching performances to the other side. I catch heat from
the stilted fire spitters on my first attempt and am pushed to a
complete retreat by the underclothed fire spinning gals onto the

familiar safety of the sidewalk. A woman dressed as a devil, fully red skinned and horned, propositions me to take a shot of pumpkin vodka. I unkindly brush her off. I am on a mission and it will take a lot more than what she has to offer to sway me from it; unless she cares to follow me back to my truck and go for a ride to the church, which I doubt she does.

There is a break coming up in the marching display just between the skeleton drummers and the slow moving donkeys that are painted goblin green and led by tribal witch doctors. This is my chance. Holding my breath I sprint across without any hiccups, besides the crowd behind me clamoring. Some are cheering me on and others spout disapproving moans.

I have made it across. A weight feels like it has been lifted from me. I was not meant to be in crowds that large and I feel as though I am breathing comfortably again. Still making haste because this mission is only a minor one. I still have more important things to attend to. The mob of people that I had seen here in the park at this town festival earlier is nowhere in sight. They have all either gone to the parade or gone home. Great for me because I do not have the time or the want to dodge the masses any more than I have tonight.

I am in the food tent alley, making my way towards the corner of the entertainment and shopping sections, when I spot a familiar face. The exotic Turkish seer walks in my direction from across the grassy footpath with rows of marquees on both sides. She moves elegantly and slow with a noticeably foreign charm in her step. The purplish headscarf she wore loosely wrapped around her head is now tied in bandana fashion, exposing more of her long voluminous black hair. The dark locks hang over her shoulder to one side just past her breasts. Her dress clings and flows to and from her body as she plucks from the popcorn box she carries. When her eyes finally meet mine she is taken back. This surprise turns swiftly into a delighted wise smirk. We finally get to arms length of each other and the Turk oracle strains to read my face for something I do not outright understand.

"Hello again. So, do you know where-" I start to say before she cuts me off in my quickness to inquire about where exactly to buy pumpkins.

"Come with me."

"I really don't have time."

She takes hold of my forearm with her ring-studded hand, dropping the popcorn onto the already littered ground, and pulls me into her velvety divining tent. On the way through the curtains her hand managed to find a way down to mine and hold it. Her thumb caresses the inside of my hand with a circling tenderness like it was searching. I do not reciprocate the affection. In fact, if I remember correctly she did say she was a palm reader. Lucky for me I do not subscribe to such fantastical beliefs. There is a certain level of delusion required to genuinely take part in or perform such fallacies. This notion promptly passes and we are again standing by the short reading table. I am only now considering how much more work I have to do just to get back to the truck and drive home. There is no reason for me to be in this tent and every second is adding to my extending night. A reasonable and acceptable amount of nerves are forming within me. I capably suppress them by telling myself the tailored motto; just go with it. Do not panic. Everything is as it should be.

I was lost in thought for, apparently, too long because when I snapped out of it the Turkish woman was taking a couple of steps backwards.

A troubled look washes over her face and she does not ask me, but tells me, "You have done something tonight."

I stare blankly at her for a few seconds as I am caught off guard by this assertion.

"Well, I walked around a bit. Saw the rest of the festival. I made it to the parade, also. It is way more intense than I ever expected," I tell her trying to sound chipper and confident.

Even someone who did not have a job requiring them to read people could see past this unnatural tone of speaking. At least enough to know something was off.

"Sit. We will drink Turkish coffee and I will read your coffee grounds."

"I'm serious. I don't have the time. I need to find pumpkins and go—" interrupted again.

This time, the disruption of my speech was caused by her outstretched hands reaching to cup my cheeks. She does this with an adoring smile and pulls herself into me for a kiss. The moment her lips touch mine, before they are really pressed against one another, an immediate wave of impassioned vigor overtakes me and I take the sides of her head into my powerful palms. She begins the fiery mashing of lips with her soft delicate hands still gently around my face. My lips do nothing but receive her passion. Then, I harness the intensity I feel to twist her head with one quick motion, sufficiently breaking her neck. She dies instantly and falls to the ground. I do not and did not have time for any of this. She was given fair warning. A necessary death to complete my urgent mission.

I can only imagine what she had planned. I also wonder what it is she was insinuating when she stated I had done something tonight. Could it be that she really did read my face with the deep searching looks she gave when first seeing me again? Was she just tenderly holding my hand or really reading my palm? The changing expressions she wore suggested all kinds of things. Or could it be that she saw the blood on my hands and considered it might not be fake?

I take the money from a wooden box on the shelf. No time to count it now but it is clearly much more than everything I have accrued tonight.

Something hangs on the wall that I had not noticed before. A blue mask of striking familiarity. I cannot place it at first, but it resonates a memory somewhere within me. I remove it from the twine it hangs from and feel its sturdiness. This mask is of quality construction. Not a plastic or rubber one like most of the people are wearing around here tonight, but of an authentic aged hardwood caliber.

A long nose, angry eyes and sharp monstrous teeth. Wait, I know it. It is the tengu captain's face who last guided me. Not exactly the same but nearly indistinguishable. The one from my now fading dream. I take the old face with me as I make my exit.

As luck would have it, there is a stall that sells pumpkins only a few tents down from the Turkish falci one. I am rather preoccupied with my thoughts as the salesman tells me about the Connecticut field pumpkin; the most common pumpkin we see used in making traditional jack-o'-lanterns and the standard variety for Halloween all together. That is about all I pick up from his explaining. I make it obvious that I do not care. After I shove a few dollars his way I pick up the uncarved medium-sized pumpkin and go. The plan was to buy a few but it seems too much hassle for anything more than this one.

I run into the same problems with the parade procession on my trek back. Unicycling witches leave no openings to cross the street. They are followed by a gapless series of undead cheerleaders and another ceaseless group of murderous robots. After the marching band of carnivorous plants, there is a break.

I cross the street with the same encouraging cheers and distasteful howls as the first time. Everybody has seen me but nobody would have the wherewithal to pick me out of a lineup or even have a reason to if, or rather, when it comes to a manhunt for the person responsible in the heinous slayings that occurred tonight.

Finally, back to the truck. I check that the duo are still soundlessly inert. They are. My gourd traveler rides shotgun next to the backpack holding Jord's head as I shift the vehicle into drive and leave. The one thing I cannot help but do is go back to the police car and the dead officer. I keep my distance but get close enough to see that he is still lying in the dim street in a pool of his own blood. The police cruiser remains untouched as well. I wish I could be here to see the town discover him and the others I left in my wake. But that is foolish thinking. I turn the truck around and leave behind a headless Jord body, a skull-fractured Nolan, a gutted Wilda and a head-bashed Myles. I will never forget the two that gifted me their unwanted interferences; the cop and the fortune teller. Goodbye Cornham, Connecticut. This has surely been a Halloween night for the books, so far. And it is not over yet.

-8-

We make it back to Elsewhere in the very late hours of night. This is no bother to me, I am just relieved to have made it home with some time before the sun comes up. It is quite a bit colder up here in the mountains than it was in Connecticut, so a fire is lit in the newly renovated and repaired Church of Elsewhere. I

144

feel dignified when considering everything I have done to
update the church and everything I have done to upgrade my
mental space. True contentment does not seem so far out of
reach anymore.

I drag the unconscious bodies of the young partiers into
the front of the church by the stage. Avery watches and permits
these actions with his silence. Monster finally comes out to see
what all the commotion is. It is hard to read a chicken for
moods, but if I had to guess, with as well as I know her now, she
is cranky. Some of the parishioners have been scratched and
pecked by the hungry hen, but otherwise, the pumpkins are their
same gloomy selves. Not much has changed since I left the
place last morning. It is warming up from the heat of the fire
now so everyone should have a more comfortable vibe,
especially me. The drive itself took a lot out of me after all the
strenuous events of the night. Being able to get warm again is a
bare minimum must.

While waiting for my guests to wake up I wrap
electrical tape around their essential appendages. Just an added
measure of restraint in addition to the cuffs. I keep the fire
stoked and stand by patiently until Olly stirs and opens his eyes.
For a moment he has no idea what is happening. Then, it seems
he has some idea. Pippa follows suit right after with the same
process. They appear to be rested but hung over. Like they slept
off one or two intoxicators but not the others. I am sure that the
ether haze within them is still lingering and probably will be for
some time.

"How do you both feel? I'll have you know that this is
the first time I've entertained more than one other person here in
my church at a time."

"Please don't kill us. Please. Please!" Olly says,
defeated.

These two are the most hopeless prey I have had here so far. Their body language and expressions scream how subdued and forlorn they are.

"Well, let's see what you can do for me first. Why don't we start with a tale. Do either of you know the history of Cornham? I'd love to hear it," I say in a mellow voice to try and instill any bit of calm into them.

The story request is not just listless small talk. I am intently interested in the history of the area.

"Don't listen to him, Olly. He's going to kill us no matter what," Pippa says while trying to sound like she is not terrified.

"There is no way you could possibly know that," matter-of-factly said by me.

Pippa looks angry but not at all like she will give me any trouble. Olly remains hope-abandoned and scared.

"I know a bit about the Cornham history. Just what they teach us in school."

"Go on, Olly. And Pippa, don't think about interrupting," I instruct while dangling the blood-crusted razor wire in front of my face.

"And you, please don't be bashful with details. Start from the very beginning," I ordered Olly.

"I don't remember exact dates, but it was sometime in the mid eighteen-hundreds that there was a cowboy named Walter Cornham. He grew up in a small lawless silver mining town in Nevada called Guardian. I think it was named by a prospector whose mine collapsed with him inside before the formation of the town. The story goes that he spent four whole days in the dark trying to get out. He dug through rocks in total darkness, not knowing if he was making a path closer to freedom or just burying himself more. Once he had given up, a silvery angel or something like that appeared to him and showed him which rocks to move to get out. He listened to it and got himself out. He said the nameless silver spirit was a miner's guardian. So he named the town Guardian to show his appreciation," Olly wipes a worried tear from his eye but is able to keep his composure.

"Very detailed, Olly. Don't become useless to me now. Continue."

"Walter Cornham was born some time after that and learned to mine and steal while he grew up around Guardian. I guess sometimes he did both at once; he would poach other peoples silver mines when they were not occupied. An outlaw named Silas Harrow took Walter under his wing at one point to teach him how to do bigger robberies in towns away from Guardian. Trains, saloons, homes, things like that. One time he was caught stealing from a home somewhere in western Utah. The landowner walked in and beat him nearly to death with a branding iron. Silas shot the man and pulled Walter to safety. They found a rock cave by a creek in Utah to hide out in for a while. Silas tended to Walter while he healed."

"How?" I ask, wanting some better imagery.

Olly made a startled jump at my interjection.

"Silas would fish the creeks and rivers, gather berries, hunt jackrabbits, keep fires burning. That kind of stuff. If I remember correctly, he was able to shoot a buffalo by their rock cave after a week of being there and that Silas was able to make sure nothing went to waste. He made smoked jerky from most of it over a bunch of different fires he built by the creek. I guess it was a huge accomplishment for one person to deal with an entire buffalo himself. I had one teacher who pointed that out. Said he tanned the hide over a fire too. And also made something called a powder horn from one of its horns; supposed to be a container to keep gunpowder dry. Can I have some water?"

"Sure, here ya go. And here you are, Pippa. Keep going, Olly. Your public speaking is getting better," I say while I pour a bit of water in each of their mouths.

It kills me to be even this cordial towards them. But this seems the best route to take with Olly. Anything harsher could cause someone as weak as him to shut down and quiet up.

"Thanks."

Pippa rolled her eyes in disgust after Olly thanked me.

"After something like two or three weeks Walter Cornham recovered enough to get moving. Silas Harrow went into the closest town. We were always told he wanted to buy a bottle of corn whisky for the road while Walter did his last bit of resting. Their plan was to leave later that afternoon. But I guess when Silas left the mercantile there was a group of people waiting for him. Lawmen mostly. The man he shot while rescuing Walter had lived and gave a description of the robbers. He was also right there with the lawmen and immediately pointed to Silas saying that he was the one who shot him. Sorry that I can't remember the man's name. I don't think it's really important though. Anyway, they were able to arrest Silas and bring him to the jail pretty easily. Silas never gave up Walter's identity. He was sentenced by the local judge to be shot at by firing squad the next day, then buried immediately afterwards. When Silas never came back, Walter went into the same town the very next day; when the execution was. Walter stumbled into the crowd not knowing what was happening, until he saw Silas standing up against a building with shackles on. The five lawmen who stood in front of Silas with their guns drawn took aim and waited for the order to shoot. Walter got all the details from the crowd about what had happened and also found out that they were still looking for the other robber. Here comes the catch. What no one knew when the order was given to fire is that the five lawmen all agreed to miss their target. Turns out, the man who the two bandits tried to rob orchestrated this. He had some pull around town because he was a respected former general for the United States military or something like that. Five shots were taken but all of them hit the wood building behind Silas. They say that Silas was super relieved because they all missed. Walter held his breath the whole time. Then, the lawmen dropped their guns and dragged Silas to the field behind the town where his grave was dug. All the people from town followed them. Everyone watched while Silas panicked and struggled in his shackles as they slowly covered him with dirt. The orders from the judge were technically followed, right? Silas was shot at, then buried right after. There were no specific instructions from the judge to shoot him to death or what to do if he was still alive after the shooting. They used this as a loophole to make Silas suffer, obviously. Walter didn't stick around to see his friend buried alive."

"The pageantry in your words is exactly what I want to hear. You're making the story come alive. Don't lose the passion."

Olly put his head down in what looks like shame. Maybe recognizing how much of a puppet he has become. Bowing to fate, he continued talking.

"Walter then headed south. He did not want to go back towards home in case he was being followed."

"Speak up, dammit! You're nearly at a whisper all of a sudden."

"Leave him alone. He's doing everything you asked and you're just fucking with him now!" Pippa orders.

She has really left me no choice now. I get up and give her a punch square to the nose. Not the hardest I possibly could but enough to tell she lost all her senses for a few seconds and enough to make her nose bleed. She makes sure not to cry out too loudly when she regains her senses. I find it pretty distasteful that I had to hit her like that but I feel there was no other choice. If I did not do something then she might feel a shift in control, something that could lead me to ending the night prematurely. Pippa whimpers quietly so that Olly can go on with the story.

"Walter Cornham made his way south. Earlier that year President Polk had officially declared war on Mexico and Walter thought that maybe the best option to hide was to join the military and disguise himself as a patriot to help the war efforts. He was stationed in Samuel, New Mexico. From there he was recruited as a dragoon to join the infantry that ended up fighting to capture the capital territory of Santa Fe, New Mexico. The Mexican-American War ended something like a year and a half later. Walter Cornham was relieved of his military duties and free to be a citizen. He decided to go back to Samuel, New Mexico, being the last familiar place he lived. His choice not to go home to Guardian in Nevada came from him wanting to give up the outlaw lifestyle. If he went back to Guardian there would be nothing waiting for him but crime. On his arrival back to Samuel there was to be a ceremony to honor those who helped in the war, something along those lines. Walter did not know it but the former general that had Silas executed had attended this ceremony. The general spotted him and told no one. He stalked Walter for a few days so he could corner him and take his own revenge on being shot in the robbery. One night he snuck into Walters tent in the Samuel Desert and pulled a gun on him. When Walter woke up he was told he was going to finish the job he started before Silas shot him. Walter was going to be tortured and killed by this man. There was a scuffle and, at some point, Walter had gotten the upper hand. Realizing that this man had come here on his own meant that probably no one else knew about him or the situation. Walter wanted the whole ordeal done with, so he shot the general in the back of the head with his own gun, killing him instantly. He dragged the body out to his campfire and dropped his head onto it to burn, with the help of some gunpowder from the buffalo powder horn Silas had made in the days before this man had him unnecessarily buried alive. This was to slow down the identification of him and the investigation, in hopes that it would buy Walter some more time to get away as far as possible. Walter packed up and rode east then north. He eventually ended up in the Connecticut woods. Just bare land with a path running through it. No one from the west pursued him and probably had no idea who he even was or what he had done. He was now in the northeast and also a stranger there."

"So, he left the Wild West behind and started a homestead in Connecticut, which led to the area and eventual town being named after him?"

"Exactly."

"How do we know this story if no one knew much about him? He must've written it down or told someone, right?"

"Yeah, I guess later in life when he had an established community and family he had told all kinds of people. It wasn't until way later that fact checkers were able to confirm that it was all true. But yeah, Cornham, Connecticut was named after him and that was his story."

Pippa chimed in with a nasally voice from the damage her nose had recently taken, "The Harrowing Parade has the double meaning of the word harrow and the last name of Silas."

I assume she offered this bit of information as a peace offering from her contentious attitude from earlier. Maybe she too now thinks there is a way out of her dismal situation and that helpfully complying is the key.

She also added, "When Walter died a lot of people said that he was poisoned by his wife and three kids. He lived to be pretty old so others never questioned his death. The family had inherited all kinds of property from this, which they used to build the community he had started into an actual town. He died on Halloween. People say he haunted his family that killed him. Each of the children died mysteriously and at a young age on different Halloween nights after that. The wife managed to be the last living one of his clan. Until she died one Halloween from choking. With a terrified confused look stuck on her face. There are so many supposedly haunted places and stories in Cornham surrounding the family."

"Very interesting history. I'll have to do some digging and see if I can find out more. You really pulled it together in this last bit, Olly. It started to sound like a proper book report there," I said, satisfied with their tale of the Cornham beginnings.

-9-

They both start to look anxious. I can only imagine what is going through their heads now that the story is over. Nerves must be guiding their imaginations on what this psychopath, who killed their friends and kidnapped them, has planned next.

Monster was sound asleep and had been throughout most of the history retelling. The jack-o'-lanterns kept their usual sedated virtue, especially The Ocean, who never cease to catch my eye in their little groups next to their bigger brethren. The candles steady the mood with a glow around pews, and the fire on the back wall of my stage maintains the warmth and light for those of us up front. Morning is just around the corner. No sunlight has begun to peak through but the somber calm before that happens is upon us. The owls and other noisy nighttime critters have quieted their voices and the early-rising morning birds have not yet started their songs.

Olly and Pippa stare at me up on my wicker chair like they are waiting for me to make a move or say something. I cannot blame them after all they have seen. I would hate to disappoint their expectations at this point. I pull the notorious backpack, that is propped by the podium, over to me. Some life develops in the hostages' eyes as I pull out Jord's severed head by his hair. This is now placed next to my chair, facing Pippa and Olly, while I get up and get the pumpkin I purchased at the Cornham Halloween festival from my truck. I ignore everyone as I cut a hole in the top of this pumpkin on the stage. The hole is not a usual hand-sized opening. Instead, I carve a hole the entire width of the pumpkin around the top. Guts and seeds are now scooped and put to the side for Monster, when she is ready for them. From here, I start to cut a big oval hole in the side of the hollowed pumpkin, roughly the size of a face. Olly seems to know where I am going with all of this and Pippa continues to gaze, unmoved, with a bloody nose. I pick up Jord's head and ease it in through the top of the pumpkin. It fits snug and firm the way a painting fits in a perfectly measured frame. His demised face is seen magnificently through the oval cutout in the pumpkin. My most realistic jack-o'-lantern yet.

"A true abomination in all its splendor. Don't you think?"

More vomiting from Olly and crying from Pippa ensues. They are smart not to answer. The response they have given is all I really wanted. They should have thought better than to take drugs from strangers. It had been the perfect catalyst in dissolving their guard. Have their parents taught them nothing? I find it droll that most everyone with kids teaches them not to take candy from strangers, except that one night a year when it is encouraged to take as much candy from as many different strangers as you can. I suppose Myles and Wilda had the presence of mind to say no and walk away. That did them no good in the end, though.

I feel inspired by fire tonight. In the past few days I have heard stories involving fires as well as seeing so much of it at the feverish Harrowing Parade in Connecticut. Here, inside the church, has an incredibly appropriate atmosphere for the occasion, but I would like to spend some time outside of it as well. Building a fire out back is an idea that calls to me right now. It also would not hurt to let these two get some rest. I induce this by strapping them both back up to the ether rigs and laying them down in front of the pews, still bound with electrical tape and handcuffs.

Out behind the church and a little ways back I begin to construct a fire. I much prefer the teepee style fire over the log cabin type of construction. With a small teepee built about knee high I now start to find bigger branches to build a larger teepee around this small one. Once that is done I go ahead and upgrade once more by finding longer logs to make an even larger teepee covering those two, making the entire wood-plenteous structure a heaping bit taller at its apex than I am. I leave the impressive unlit bonfire to wait for when I am ready. With the ether stricken visitors still under the chemical spell, I sit above them in my chair and open big holes in the bottoms of one rotting Blue, one rotting Zipper and one rotting Ghost from the crowd. The Ocean do not seem to mind that I have not chosen any of them.

Olly and Pippa awaken outside with their backs to the unlit teepee of wood and decaying jack-o'-lanterns on their heads like masks. It is a slimy mess inside of those jack-o'-lanterns. The outside skin that was once firm and slick is now mushy to the touch. The flesh inside turns to muck when handled. I had to be very delicate when cutting the holes in the bottoms and just as delicate when slipping them on my guests heads. Now that they are realizing once again what is going on, Olly speaks up through the stitch patterned mouth of his Zipper mask.

"I can barely see anything for fucks sake."

Pippa, in her Blue mask, chimes in right after with, "Can barely hear anything either."

For how snug the gourds fit it makes sense that their hearing is muffled and sight eclipsed in the lines of their vision.

They both sit on the ground facing away from the campfire, that they have no way of knowing is behind them, and with no easy way to turn around. It is still dark outside and rather cold. I think about removing their bindings because they certainly have nowhere to run or the necessary capability, given their state.

I turn to Blue and say, "Pippa, you were so eager to declare earlier that there are numerous ghost stories around Cornham. Let's hear one."

It is hard to tell what her expression was saying through the pumpkin, but her tone was of reluctance.

"Fine. Sure. The one that we always talked about when we were young is the haunted waterfall everyone calls Guardian Falls. They call it that because kids hike miles out into these woods to the mediocre waterfall with a swimming hole at the bottom. Claim they see the mining ghost thing that the prospector saw and named the town of Guardian after; the place Walter Cornham was from. Some time in the nineteen-seventies three different kids died there. All within a month. It's always been kind of a mystery and talked about as a haunted place a lot. That good enough, you fucking psycho?"

I loathe the lack of details she gave and how she did not even mention how the kids died or what the stories they tell about them are. I detest the last comment as well. What I do savor about her response is my non-immediate reactiveness to it. I can identify more and more lately how the previous me would have ripped her apart the second she finished that last comment. The unavoidable urge would have taken over and Olly would have gone down with her. I have been trying my hardest to pinpoint what exactly has changed within me lately. Every time I consider this I think I have it more narrowed down. It feels like the root of my resilience towards waves of, normally, overpowering emotions is simply just my current station in life. I have my Elsewhere Church. I have my pumpkin friends; whom I know are not actually real by most any definitions, but have become real enough in other ways to help with my feeling of fulfillment and contented spirit. My hobbies, such as what I am doing presently, are enhanced immeasurably by the agitated shackles I have broken free from. There is that old trope in movies or television and even real life, that when there is someone who cannot handle their own emotions, someone else gives the advice of walking away or telling them to just breathe. That is all easier said than done when you are not satisfied with your current life circumstances. If I am dissatisfied with most things around me and in me then why should I hold back letting that dissatisfaction affect others? Let the irrational behavior be my excuse for not thinking things through and inevitably cause added dissatisfaction. That is how my subconscious used to let me handle things. Now I understand that you need to be self-satisfied by whatever means necessary. For me, it was running away and finding this place. I can now do what I love without inner hindrance. I can profoundly harm others without the rue afterwords.

Pippa and Olly have been staring at me with the droopy pumpkins on their heads for long enough. We all have been sitting in silence since Pippa's abrupt ending to her story.

"Pippa, no. That was not good enough."

I reach behind my back and pull forward the Ghost pumpkin that I had put a hole in the bottom of just moments before. I place it in front of my legs and face it towards the occupied Zipper and Blue ones before me. It takes them a second but they both simultaneously see that Ghost is occupied as well. They focus and scan the inside of Ghost's eyes and see a pair of humanly familiar ones. These eyes are Jord's. He has been upgraded to fit inside a Ghost. They must now be connecting all sorts of dots in their heads. Are we to be ornaments inside a pumpkin like our friend? Is that why these pumpkins are on our heads now?

The choice to remove Jord's head from the blank oval-holed pumpkin was easy. If Zipper and Blue both got tenants then why would Ghost not have one? The open oval one will have to be used for something else.

"I won't hesitate to hit you again."

"Just kill us already! What's the point of all of this? We're already scared."

"I will definitely be killing you, Pippa. Do you want to be beaten also? There's all sorts of ways to make this worse for everyone, if you care to go that route."

She snivels for a moment, which I allow without rushing. She has long since accepted defeat, so she does not need much time to drag out crying over this anymore.

"Okay, you want more details about the story?"

"Yes. Tell me."

"No one knows for sure what happened to these kids, by the way. But, some of the other kids that went with them say that the ones who died were almost in a hypnotized way when they climbed up the waterfall and jumped head first into the rocks below. I forgot to mention, on all three separate occasions these kids died the same exact way. Their friends say the possessed ones mumbled about seeing a silvery spirit out there in the water that told them to climb the waterfall and let their heads soar into the rocks below. They all used the word 'guardian' at some point in their enchantment too."

"Pretty spooky for children to hear about, I take it?"

"Yeah, that one was the scariest for us. We still always went out there and played the Taunting Game."

"Taunting Game? Go on."

"Oh, yeah. It's when you swim out to the middle of the swimming hole below the falls and stand on the Taunting Rock, that's what we call it, and then beg the guardian silvery spirit to reveal itself to you. You taunt it by calling it bad names and all that. If you're one of the brave kids you pretend to be possessed and climb the waterfall and act like you're going to jump into the rocks below. Like the kids who died did."

"That was way better, Blue."

"Blue?" Pippa says, confused.

"Pippa. I mean Pippa."

10

I give Pippa and Olly a real intent look and examine the Blue and Zipper faces they wear, albeit spoiled decomposing faces. Embodied, like in my dreams. I have flashes of them each grabbing a leg of mine before throwing me off a sailing ship. And before that, they both insisted I see the captain of that ship. Then it occurs to me that I have that captain's face, in mask form, or a close enough version of it. I run into the church and fish it out of my backpack. I put it on myself before returning to the pumpkin-headed victims. All of us now wear disguises, true to the Halloween spirit. Olly is comatose by the looks of him. I wonder if being inside that pumpkin gives him a tiny sense of protection. He cannot hear or see enough for a sensory overcharge. Protected in his head cocoon, he just has to sit there and wait. Pippa is more alert. Probably because I have been making her engage in the storytelling. Or possibly, it is a bewildering fright as to why I have a Japanese demon mask on my face.

I feel empowered in the mask. Not myself. I guess that is the point in dressing up for Halloween in the first place; to be and feel and act like whatever creature you disguise yourself as. In some ways, I have always been a creature disguised as a human, a normal functioning human.

The daylight is about to start poking through the veil of this dark cold night. I have thoroughly enjoyed my exploits in the shadowy darkness, but am ready to bring this Halloween escapade to an end. Monster, the typical early riser, has joined us in our clearing back behind the church. She approaches us hesitantly as she stops to eye the embodied pumpkins with every other step she takes. After a few confusing pauses to scrutinize the animated and vocal rotting vegetables, she relaxes and goes about her business of scratching around in the leaves.

"Your heads will be cut off and used to decorate my church," I say low and humble, as if they should be proud that their mutilated bodies will be a part of my decor.

This is not my actual expectation, that they should be proud. I just wanted to keep the dread looming within them with my coolness about the situation at hand. They still have no idea about the campfire built just behind them. There was no opportunity or ability to turn around to see it or spot it through their peripherals, which are limited from inside the pumpkins.

"You two have had a long night. Much longer than I normally allow. And for sticking with me all this time I will leave it up to you."

"What do you mean?" asks Olly and Zipper.

"Pippa, do you have any idea what I'm talking about?"

"He's going to ask how we want to be killed, Olly."

Olly then repeats, "No. No, no. No, no. No no no," over and over at different volumes. A futile surrendering plea for release.

I calmly walk over to Olly and strangle him. Not to death, though. As I press my grips together around his throat his bound-together hands jolt up and try to break my hold on him. He hits my chin a few times as his one combined fist goes through the gap between my arms. I am close enough to get a good look at his eyes, which I could not do from where I was sitting a moment ago, and they are wide, wild and fearful inside Zippers differently proportioned oval eye holes. He writhes on the ground, not ready to forfeit his existence without a fight. I let go. He is alive. I saved his life by stopping the deathly throttling I embraced him with. A true testament to the restraint I have learned to impose on my urges; or perhaps proof to a total disintegration of my urges. He coughs uncontrollably and hard enough to gag. Pippa attempts to keep her composure by gently rocking back and forth.

I find it hard to get rid of these two. Not because I feel some sort of guilt about killing them or attachment to them whatsoever, but because I am not quite sure how I want them to die. Maybe I should go ahead and give them choices like I planned to before choking Olly.

"Okay, so how would you like to go? I can strangle you to completion or, perhaps, burn you alive? How about just start cutting pieces off with a handsaw until you bleed out? Maybe gut you like Wilda? I sure wouldn't mind pulling out your innards and draping them around the church like tinsel. Christmas is just around the corner."

Pippa struggles to say, "Can you please just make it quick instead of any of that?"

Olly coughs and cries saying, "Please just let us go."

I wish they would just not ask to be let go. The likelihood of anyone in their situation being let go by someone in my situation is absurd. Asking something like that is completely unrealistically hypothetical and should not be entertained. As if I would hear the suggestion and all of a sudden agree with granting release. Olly has increasingly become less and less use to me because of the blinders he wears about his situation. He is disillusioned and it takes away from my experience.

"Olly, I think I have something for you," I say this, not really knowing exactly what that something is yet.

I get up and walk over to the back of my truck to look for something that pops out to me. While doing this, I try to create and take on a demented personality of the demon tengu mask I wear. An old rusty railroad spike that is randomly in my toolbox calls to me for this exact situation. I take that and my hammer over to Olly. Very swiftly, I put it in front of his right eye and tap it with the hammer before he ever had a chance to react. I did not bang the thing hard enough to go straight through his head. Just a quick tap so that the railroad spike pierces and pops his eye into a mush. He throws his head side to side in pain and confusion. I kick him backwards to the ground and push down on his throat with my foot. This holds him somewhat still so I can nudge the railroad spike into the other eye with another fast peck of the hammer. I get the same result with the left eye as I did with the right, a pulpy sludge. He yells as loud as his vocal cords will allow. Confusion is no longer the right way to describe the blind Olly's state; complete stupefaction is more appropriate now. He does not know anything in this moment. His usefulness, at least at an entertainment level, is climbing. Pippa cries and yells with him in her jack-o'-lantern head shroud, while I cackle a forced laugh behind my fiend mask. I want to silence him now. I try my hardest to grab his tongue while he yells. He bites me powerfully. I should have seen this coming and also cannot blame him for it.

I take a quick moment to point out to myself that the former me would have flown into a rage and hurt him all kinds of ways for that one. But, I am enlightened and cultivated now. I appreciate the situation from all angles. I react on an intentional level, instead of a bothered one. The results on this will not be much different, except for the fact that I am not agitated.

I remove the Zipper jack-o'-lantern from his head. He continues wailing just the same. The spike gets placed under his chin in the fleshy part between both sides of the mandible. I give it a harder whack than the eyes, enough to pierce straight through into his mouth so it hits his tongue. I now have control of his head via the railroad spike through his jaw. His screams dampen and head is held still. I reach into a pocket with my free hand and pull out my folding knife. After flicking it open in a smooth assertive motion I make a few deep irregular cuts on both sides of his cheeks, just under and in front of his ears. Then a few more deeper ones under the very back of his jaw, where it hinges. An abundance of blood is exiting his mouth and face wounds while the eyeless man bellows out in agony. I count out three profound breaths and then crank the lodged railroad spike to the right, causing a cracking sound in Olly's jaw, also making it sit broken and uneven now. Then I pull up away from his face, ripping the entire jaw out with the spike. It is disconnected from the hinges and only stays linked to the man by some neck skin and tendon. These links are now cut and I hold the severed jaw in my hand by the affixed railroad spike. Olly begins to choke on his blood. Pippa falls over and cries harder. Olly stops moving. Dead, jawless and eyeless with his unsupported tongue hanging low.

Pippa has gone in full fight or flight mode. She clenches up and tries to break free of the handcuffs and electrical tape that restrains her. She must know that there is no way out of this. Her struggling is all mental and subconsciously suggested. What else can she do but try?

My spirit is soaring. I cannot stop myself from going back to the thought that this night could not be going any better. I am flourishing, both mentally and psychically. I am thankful to myself for having pushed me to leave college to pursue a true passion. I would still be back studying and doing homework and probably avoiding Halloween parties if I had not decided to take steps towards leaving my comfort zone and eventually finding the Elsewhere Church. I would be driving myself crazy on a regular basis always wondering 'what if' and 'what else'.

"Well, Pippa. Just you and me now."

Pippa has checked out. She is not all there, and that means she will be no more fun on a back-and-forth level. She is crying and I imagine that this is all she will be useful for from now on; and I personally have no use for that. Something tells me there are better ghost stories about Cornham, but I guess I may never know them, for now.

I go get my handsaw and grind it through Olly's neck to remove his maimed head. When that is done I move a cluster of wood pieces from the fire structure in order to place his headless carcass in the center. Pippa does not turn to see this and is still unaware of the towering teepee behind her. When he is sufficiently in the heart of his new housing I go and fetch a long thick tree trunk that I cut down weeks ago. One that I have not gotten around to chopping into smaller pieces for firewood. This tree trunk is the heaviest thing I have had to move all night. It takes me a good amount of strength and time to roll it over to the wood teepee. When I get there I muster up any and all power within me to stand it up on the edge and slightly inside the fire structure. It is thick enough to have good footing and stability to not fall over without some more muscle. I fix my toothy, wild-eyed demon mask that was jostled in the tree hauling so that it is straight over my face again. Pippa is then grabbed by the neck and sat snug up against this tree trunk. Her legs stretch outwardly, away from the teepee tower and still bound together. I cut her hands free and pull them behind her to wrap them around the tree as far as they will extend, in a sort of backwards hug. Then, I wrap some of that razor wire, used to behead her friend Jord, around a wrist. A length of it is then stretched around the tree through the space that leads to her other hand, on which more of the razor wire is wrapped around. Thus, creating razor wire handcuffs. I stuff the series of teepees with dry dead leaves starting with the center kindling one. A bit of gasoline is splashed around it for good measure, too. When I give Pippa the chance to speak any final words she just cries and starts to hyperventilate.

I hear a faint strained, "Fuck you," or, "I hate you."
Impossible to tell exactly what she is saying.

I was hoping she would say something compelling before I burned her alive, like the Brewer Witch and her elf cup anecdote. But she did not. I expected too much. People had an exceedingly more creative way with words in the past, but those days are gone. Common creativity is a thing of history. It is left for those who seek and study it rather than regular folk these days. Television and musicians absorb our creatives and drain the creativity out of those who get sucked in and addicted to their creations. It leaves them not needing to be inventive because, to them, someone else has already done the work. But before modern day audio and video recordings were around, all people must have had this blossoming poetic nature inside of them in order to get those urged artistic needs met. Now, instead of saying something compelling before you die, you draw a blank thought and leave the rest of us with no great quip to wrap up the end of your story after you are gone. A potentially inspired quote from them, that may have lived on through the ages, has no way of being birthed into existence. The possibility smothered by a life of underdeveloped poeticism and imagination.

I light the fire with a match. It goes up in a ravishing inferno. There is a good mix of dead seasoned wood from the forest and fresher unseasoned wood, like the recently chopped maple trunk that Pippa is fastened to.

I cannot see Pippa's hands and wrists but they are surely bloodied by now with all the wiggling she is doing. The smoke hits her in waves as the barely noticeable breeze must be constantly changing course. The most alluring part about this right now is the sun starting to illuminate the sky, very lightly. The past few minutes it has been a dim watery blue color. Now, it is bringing on all shades of dark purple and vibrant neon orange. At the peak of the attractive features in the early morning sky, my rotting pumpkin-headed Pippa coughs. A little bit at first then gradually more. Her arms start to bubble and darken. The mushy face of the jack-o'-lantern, Blue, starts to warp glumly now, too.

Before her head is totally ruined, and before I even know if Pippa is dead or not, I remember I wanted to save everything above her neck for decoration. I run to the back of the Elsewhere Church and grab my axe. I use a light jogging stride on the short trip back to the bonfire in order to get a forceful swing at Pippa's blistering neck with my sharp axe. It goes clean through her neck, a direct hit, and gets stuck in the maple totem she is propped up against. The head popped off smooth and freely. When it landed on the ground, however, the pumpkin which contained it split in a few spots which made it collapse a bit. I have no other option but to pull it open and extract Pippa's head. Fortunately, I have more of Blue to make a container out of. The last thing that this girl ever saw, assuming she was still alive and conscious, was a Japanese demon face pacing toward her with an axe in a ready to swing position. And swing it did.

I watch the fire burn my guests until the sun has lit up the sky. No more morning purple or orange, just light blue and white clouds. I sit in front of the fire with total tranquility while wrapping electric tape around Olly's head and jaw to keep everything in one piece. It then goes back into Zipper. All three heads are brought inside the church where Monster went hiding as soon as the fire was lit. I do not have the energy to open up another Blue to jam Pippa's head inside. This will have to wait until the morning, or rather, evening or next morning, as it is already well into this morning.

The last thing that goes through my mind is that I forgot to check Olly's wallet before sending it to the flames along with his headless body.

-11-

I am brought back to life from itchiness. Not itchy like a rash, more like bunches of tiny soft pins are gently scratching at my skin through my clothes. When I shake off the fuzziness that held my perception I realize that I am laying in grass. I stand up to collect my head and the urge to itch goes away. Around me is an unending garden that goes on forever in almost every direction. The sky and air are a light grey with a dusty overcast above. All of the flowers, herbs, shrubs and grass are a blueish grey, as far as I can see. I walk in the direction to where the massive garden seems to break in the distance. Plots staked out with tiny fencing to separate the different plant species go by, one after another after another, on my disoriented stroll. The roses here, which I am used to seeing as red and occasionally some other brilliant color, are all this shade of Prussian blue-grey. Their stalks, normally an earthy green, are grey also. Same as with the leaves. Same with the grass. Also the boxwood shrubs that endlessly maze through the landscape, grey. The rhododendron, the monkey cups, poppies, daffodils, sumac, raspberry bushes, orchids; all this smokey shade of drab coloring. Every single plant that surrounds me, all grey.

My head is swimming with puzzlement while I turn around to see if there is any other tint to be found on this sooty shaded landscape. There is not. I do catch sight of a moving figure off in the distance from where I came from. Without any knowledge of where I am or going or what it is that I am supposed to be doing, I double back in the direction of the figure. It is a feminine shape wearing a tattered murky black sundress. She sports a floppy wide-brimmed harvest hat the same color as her dress. It gracefully veils most of her face as she smells a grouping of flowers upon my approach. I open my mouth to speak but she beats me to the dialogue.

"These. Beautiful aren't they?"

I know what she is saying but it takes me a moment to understand it. Everything now seems to be in slow motion. My perspective of things went from crisp clear focus of the material around me, though dull, to clouded and splotchy. Now like a watercolor painting that used only grey tones. The woman turns around and it is Eeka. I am no longer surprised when she appears like this. She plucks a flower from in front of her and holds it to my nose. I feel like it is me who is in slower pacing than everything else, which is in slow motion to begin with.

"Middlemist's Red," Eeka says, then picks a few more of the foggy grey bloom.

Clearly, this is the name of the flower she gathers. She lifts her head up and extends it back a bit in order to bypass the hat flop that obstructs her view.

With her nose turned up and eyes fixed on mine she murmurs, "You must always follow me. What I say. It's for the good of us both."

A tear drips from the corner of her eye, down her cheek, and she lowers her head once more to hide her face with the slacked rim of her dark sunhat. A tear rolls down my face in the same way. Eeka's hair is much darker than the first time I saw her. It is a seemly black that accents the grey contrast of our surroundings. She points a finger towards where I was walking a moment ago. A trail of sparkling grey followed her arm in a blur as she lifted it up to do this, reminiscent of trails I have seen on LSD hallucinations. This startles me for no apparent reason and I am nearly launched into an internal panic. I say my mollifying phrase out loud instead of inside my mind like I usually do.

"Don't panic. Everything is as it should be. Can't change anything and everything is fine."

Eeka's face starts out with an understanding expression for acceptance of this response, then harshly changes to an impatient one. She then grasps the scruff hair on the back of my head and pushes me forward in the direction she had just been pointing. There is no anger or offense taken. The mood is still strangely light and filled with bland wonderment. I feel no hostility coming from her, even as she takes this aggressive action.

The obvious hint is taken and I begin the trek in my originally started direction. It begins to feel more and more like being in a painting the further I get. The breezy movement of the grass and plants slows gradually to a stop and it all stays in a fixed position, except for me, who continues walking. The view of everything is less sharp and distinct and becomes more blotched and smeared.

When I get nearer to the end of this expansive garden a little white building with a door comes into my sight. This surely must be where I am supposed to go because there is nothing else but fields of plant life around. The sectioned plant life begins to taper off and I see less and less of it. The space is now occupied with rows and rows of cages. Not little ones, large ones with thick metal bars like you would see in the zoo to hold bears or lions. These cages are empty, however. To the left and right of me are the janky remnants of an abandoned zoo that give off an eerie temper. One that I strive to have for the Elsewhere Church. It was not until I heard the faint roars inexplicably coming from a distance that I realized it was dead silent since I have been here, save for the interaction with Eeka. Could these animal shouts be coming from escaped beasts? Certainly I should be able to see them in one direction or another, given there is nothing big enough to obstruct my view. It does not make sense, but I know to just go with it. Everything is how it should be. The door to the little white building is now right in front of me. Crystal clear unlike the rest of the distorted landscape all around me. I grab and turn the doorknob but there is no sensation that feels like I am touching anything at all. Looking down at my hand to make sure I am actually turning the knob and opening the door, I can tell that everything is progressing as it should. It just feels like nothing while I do it. Just a ghost opening a door.

Bright radiant lights gleam when I enter through the doorway. An enormous room with colorful carpeting of purple, orange, black and yellow paisley design that pops. Tall ceiling with white ivory wavy shapes carved into it. Tables topped with smooth green felt, some with a spinnable checkered wheel laying at one end of them. Machines with bright lights of all different colors and images with stools in front of each one. I am in a casino. The size of the building I am in now could not possibly be the one I saw from the outside. But, here I am, alone wandering the vacant casino. It no longer feels like a painting but like I am now inside an ethereal illusion.

The relief from colors coming back to view is matched by the relief of more noises being present. I hear the pings and chimes of slot machines near and distant. The roulette wheel spinning and clacking the little ball that pops around it to find its prosperity-deciding home, though no one is manning any of the ones I can see. The din of gambling addicts and swanky chatter is encompassing, yet there is not a body to be seen.

I make slow progress through the rows of uninhabited poker tables. Progress is made deeper and deeper into this poker section of the massive gambling hall and I end up in a sea of these games. All directions have long ranges and rows with the green felted tops. I remember to go with whatever flow this is and end up coming upon an occupied card game. My stomach feels light, this is about the only sensation I can tap into at the moment. Eeka stands behind the table, wearing her same tattered black sundress as in the garden, and deals her three seated orange faced patrons on the other side their cards. She then waves me over, inviting me to sit and play with the familiar betters. Zipper, Blue and Ghost sit and focus on the game in their most distinguished form I have seen them as yet. Classic black tuxedo suits with deluxe black bow ties and orange pocket squares. Their postures are dignified and they have top tier etiquette.

"You are quite welcome to have a seat here," Ghost states as he gestures to a seat between him and Blue.

"Yes, please take this seat between us," says Blue.

I accept and sit. I realize now that I have never been this lucid when being around these embodied three. Nor have I been this physically close without them forcibly trying to get rid of me. Normally, some high level of confusion or not knowing what is happening consumes me while I try to stay relaxed and focused in their presence. There is no trying at the moment. I genuinely feel confident being here. It is hard to say why I have such a coherent state. My guess is that I am getting more used to being in these situations now, with these beings. I have proper expectations with them, even when it comes to the mysterious nature of their visit. Also, I have somewhat cognitive memories of them. With my now logical thought process, there are a few questions I would like to ask.

"Do you remember throwing me off that ship into The Ocean?"

"Fold. Of course we do," Zipper replies from the end of the table as he pushes his cards forward then fixes his bowtie.

"When it's time to go it's time to go. You must learn this," Blue adds.

I find it comforting to see these three with ripe heads. At least as fresh and firm as the day I carved them. I am now so used to the rotting and darkened look that their kind sports now. These visits that they accord me are a reminder of what they once were and will be again someday.

"And if I don't know when it's time to go, you guys will be there to grab me and throw me into uncertainty, I take it?" I say with a hint of restrained bitterness.

"Maybe not us. In all likelihood, someone or something, though. I call."

"I call, as well."

"Call. We applaud the new additions to Elsewhere. The captain should be pleased."

"About the captain, where is he? Who is he?" another question from the list in my head.

"An expected question, but an unresolvable one by us. All in," Ghost declares and pushes all his poker chips into the betting pile.

"Who can answer it then?"

The bright casino lights that filled the room began to dim and darken. All qualities of the general mood did the same. The three pumpkin-headed gamblers slowly went from their upright respectable sitting posture to hunched up gargoyles, with arches in their backs and shoulders that chill me to the core. They look forward in Eeka's direction but with lightly downward-bowed heads. Their faces drop in a maddened and provoked way. My heart is starting to race. I look from side to side next to me and their dispositions are eclipsing into something menacing. Had I spoken too much? It is futile to try and make sense of these pumpkins. Everything is one way and then it is another an instant later. There is most likely some way to decipher their puzzling ways. For now, I must accept that I am far from solving their ethos.

Their individual and separately specific facial features have all turned to ominous scowls of brooding impression. I push my seat back and start to stand up, as it feels now I am way too close for comfort. They stay fixed in the sitting positions with straightforward glares. I look up at Eeka and she motions, with her chin and a raise of her eyebrows, a pointing nod in the direction behind me. A clear and subtle hint to be on my way. It is time to go. Best to take my exit now before the inevitable snap that is about to happen with Zipper, Blue and Ghost. Realizing that there is no telling exactly what they are capable of, I make haste to leave those three morose creatures and Eeka behind in their curious ambience. After turning around, I see there is a door directly behind me. I take my last look at them and go. Again, I do not feel the doorknob as I hold and twist it open.

       I burst to an upright sitting position in my sleeping bag on the stage of the church. My heart is pumping and cold sweat covers me. I have slept most of the day away and can see the late afternoon sun turning into the evening sun from the window on the wall. All of the Ghosts and Blues and Zippers stare at me and this gives me an uneasy but comforting feeling, both at the same time. Slightly tense, but in a way that is filtered through familiarity, which comes out as this reassuring sensation I feel. I do not dwell on them or The Ocean right now. Instead, I pull out my journal from underneath my pillow and write down this dream before it deserts me.

-12-

I fell back to sleep shortly after awakening from the dream. It is now the morning after that, which means that if I fell asleep right after the bloody morning bonfire and am waking up the very next morning then I have had a marathon of rest. Slept an entire day through, only waking up that one time, briefly. I desperately have to expel fluids. I desperately need to ingest fluids. Once both are done I check on Monster. I consider how I have not dropped food for her in at least a day, but also know she is capable of foraging on her own. Whether it be outside or through my food supply, which I leave available to her if she needs.

Still shaking off the sleep as I peek into her nesting spot under the front pew. She is not there, as usual for the morning time. But, to my unexpected delight, she has laid her first egg. A medium-sized white egg with a slightly pink tint. This has barely crossed my mind, eggs. It is hard not to consider the providential timing of this achievement. After spending a whole long night gratifyingly hacking up six young Halloween partiers, one foolish cop and one questionable foreign charlatan, I am rewarded by my Monster and the universe with this egg. A representation of sustenance for me. A gift to tell me I am doing something right, that I can consume and it will provide nourishment for me to keep living and pursuing my endeavors fueled from the nutriment I receive. If ever there was a doubt in my mind about the path I am following, this egg has answered everything I need to know. The very sight of it and the reassuring message it has given has sufficiently brought me back to life from my long slumber.

Monster comes back in through her Monster door on the side of the wall and eyes me for a second as I pull the egg out of her nest. I keep my eye on her because I am curious to how she will react to this. This is new to both of us. As much as I hate to admit that I, a loner and irrational sociopath, turned relatively centered psychopath, now share this space with another being; it is true. For any excuse I could have for ridding her of this place, I can never argue the fact that she now provides for it. A moment of quizzical looks from her turns right into her going about her business. Scratching around and scanning the floor for food, without a care regarding me taking her first laid egg.

I make some coffee to sip on while cooking this divine gift. The egg is cracked on the side of my pan that I have buttered and heated up over the stone fireplace. It goes in undisturbed and whole. The shell is thrown in the fire for convenience. I let it fry a bit before popping the yolk with the corner of my spatula. The yolk spreads out a little and I help it evenly cover the white with a shake of the pan and a few flicks of the spatula. I do not mix them as one would do to make scrambled eggs. No, this is simply a fried egg with a delay on breaking the yolk. This is my preferred method for cooking eggs above all other ways. Normally I would add a pinch of salt and a lot of freshly cracked black pepper, but I do not add anything for this one. I want to taste the egg unobscured. Monster is dropped a few little bits and pieces while I devour the rest. No complaints from either of us. I sit in my wicker chair and she scratches about on the stage around me.

It is then that I have to ask, "Monster, did you lay this the other night when I was tending the fire? You were outside with me and the guests and then early in the bonfire scene you showed yourself back inside. I assumed you were scared of the blaze, like most animals are, but maybe you were also laying that egg. Oh well, I'll probably never know for sure. But, I'm okay with sticking to that story. You, preparing an offering for the first time after my long night of magnificent intensity."

She gives no answer or anything I could possibly reach for as a response.

The cold spells are apparently still snapping back and forth as today is turning out to be one of the warmer days this autumn. The one egg from Monster was not enough to fill me up after nearly two days of not eating. I am thankful to have anticipated this on the morning of Halloween when I overstuffed myself with food. Otherwise, I might legitimately categorize my situation as starving. Cooked grits and bananas that are just about to start browning are shoveled into my mouth. Monster was thrown a small handful of the grits before I cooked them. She was also given the banana peels, which she fancies pulling the stringy bits off of and eating.

Sufficiently full and energized, I get to work on my decorations. Pippa's head was without a home still, so that is first on the list. I chose her first one poorly, in the heat of the moment. It was way too rotted and did not stand a chance against the activities of the night. I grab a Blue from one of the middle pews that looks to be sturdier than most of her twins about the church. Cutting easily into the top of this one, enlarging the hole so it is big enough to drop the head of this young lady in, I recall back on how congenial carving the fresh ones are for me and yearn for when I can do this again in large quantities. I can just imagine these pews and walls and stage and outside littered with fresh jack-o'-lanterns all at once. This old black Elsewhere Church will be adorned with pumpkins of orange and white and blue or whatever other colors I can find out there. Perhaps I can start pumpkin seeds early this coming spring. I can make a space with huge potential for growing my own pumpkin patch in a clearing by the church.

The head fits in perfectly. With my three headful friends, two rotting and one ripe, ready to be displayed, I can only think of one spot that makes sense. Under the front pew on the opposite side of the aisle where Monster's nest is. They will not be crowding Monster there, but will also be close enough so that when the maggots start to populate the meat she will have easy access to protein-filled treats. They are also greatly visible from my stage.

PART FOUR

-1-

November flew by. My truck has proven itself worthy in the mountain snow. It had gotten stuck a few times, but managed to pull itself out in every instance. No sliding and always starts right up after sitting cold for days. Firewood has lasted me, and it should continue to last throughout the next month or two if I can continue the pacing in which I am burning it. I might have to adjust this technique or, more probably, continue chopping wood to stay on top of my slowly shrinking stack to get through to spring.

I have not gone out and found any more guests for the church yet. I believe I am still getting by off of the high from Halloween night, a month ago now. That is not to say that I have not gone into peoples homes a few times at night, to creep through their bedrooms while they sleep and take what cash I can find. I do not have much need for anything other than money right now. There was one time that I had taken some canned food. Another time, when I realized that boredom would set in once it got too cold to do anything up here, I ended up in the house of an elderly woman in the middle of the night. I took a book from a box of literature she had tucked away in her basement. It is titled Paresthesiac by Baxter W. Ripper, written in eighteen sixty-seven. I am not quite halfway through reading it but so far it has held my attention and makes me wish I took more from her hidden packed up library. I will have to make another stop there sometime soon. The book tells the story of a man that has the ability to induce the feeling of pins and needles; that prickling feeling you get beneath the skin when limbs fall asleep or go numb. Through a ritual he performed to gain this power, from an ancient forgotten demonic god, he can create this sensation just by touching someone. When he does this, the tingling sensation gradually gets more intense and unshakable. Finally, it feels as though actual pins and needles are harshly poking through the skin which causes very real rips in his victims flesh until they basically tear open enough to bleed out in agony. The very beginning started off slow, but quickly turned brilliant; this is something I can relate to. If I could find ten or fifteen more books by this fellow I would be set until spring.

The church is holding up fine, without any major leaks or damage of any kind. When I notice a significant enough leak or draft coming from any gaps in the wood it is hastily patched up with scrap wood I collect each time I go into town. The snow has dumped down here and there, but not enough to barricade me in. If that happens I can climb up through a window and shovel myself out from there. Hard to say exactly how I would handle that until it actually happens, though. Monster has steadily been providing us three eggs a week. A number I hope will increase when it gets warmer, but have no real problems if it stays the same. The horde of gourds that sit in the pews are now all collapsed in on themselves, except for a couple that have held strongish, but I suspect their ruin is just around the corner.

Jord, Pippa and Olly, who I now call Ghost, Blue and Zipper have been moved outside, a short walk from the church. The fetid smell was overwhelming. If I had a bigger supply of formalin, the preserving chemical that still holds those green Avery eyes inside the Avery jack-o'-lantern upon the podium, I would certainly make arrangements for them to be floating in jars. It is a nice walk to go visit them on their three stumps, though. They give the edge of the snowy forest a haunting quiet charm.

Today I must drive down into Saint Ox for groceries. The fire is filled with enough wood to keep it warm until I get back. Monster will stay behind, as usual, and keep an eye on things. The way down and through the mountain is wet and snowy, but not terrible. The roads around Saint Ox are plowed, though even if they were not it would be fine. The snow is only around ankle height down here, and it is not even twice as high up at the Elsewhere Church.

My groceries are bought for the week at the local market. Same as always. Along with a copy of the local paper. With the cold weather it is easier to keep things refrigerated by just placing it in or on top of the snow. Normally, I could not buy things like meat or eggs without having to eat them immediately. One more luxury I have to remind myself of while not being able to carve pumpkins.

This morning is different, however, because I did not eat breakfast before heading into town. When this happens, and I am around so many establishments that sell food, it is punishing even trying not to consider paying for someone else to cook for me. I have never made a habit of going out to eat, especially because I do not care to be around other people in general. When hunger is involved I have recently learned to ignore my comfort triggers and give in to entertaining ideas for other methods of dining. Today I gave in to the hunger and decided to stop at The Buzzy Bee Diner. Having been here once before, I knew it was a solid option to quell my craving for pancakes. I seat myself at the kitchen bar counter by the griddle station, same as last time. Nothing has changed since I was last here. Nineteen-fifties retro vinyl on most of the furniture. Old ads posted up all over the walls. Nickel jukeboxes for the tables. The impish devil, that answers crucial questions for ten cents by producing a card for the payer, sits in front of me once more. Another familiar face approaches. The large greasy man, who took my order last time I was here, has not changed one bit. In appearance or demeanor. Stained white shirt and bothered attitude. I order the stack of pancakes and carrot juice.

"Jayne Mansfield. Orange root," he yells in no particular direction and with an increased look of being bothered.

I had forgotten all about the pancakes being called 'Jayne Mansfield' here. This time, I remember to ask about it.

"Hey, so why are the pancakes called a Jayne Mansfield?"

"How the hell should I know? They've been saying it here since my father opened the place. Far as I know, a lot of other people call them that too."

I am immediately reminded of how I felt last time I was here, well over a month ago, and how I impulsively wanted to gut this man for the sour look he gave me. This time, he went as far as firing back at me, almost implying the very question was appalling. There is no doubt in my mind that I could carve this greasy man up like a pig, but I have no intent to. There would be nothing artful about it. Revenge should not be the motive. The very act would be a sort of hasty retribution that I do not care to indulge in anymore.

I do not respond at all to the man. He brings my pancakes and carrot juice without a word as he hands it over, and I respond accordingly by also saying nothing. He had no answer for me about the Jayne Mansfield pancakes conundrum. I guess not all things can be answered. Some information in life is simply not accessible and this needs to be accepted. While I am eating I overhear one of the waitresses conversing with the rude griddle cook.

"Did you hear there's a break in the Avery Fletcher case? They have a witness who came forward yesterday."

"Goddamn. Took them long enough."

"Well, I guess the witness saw a youngish man leaving her house, or entering it. I can't remember all the details but it's all in the paper."

I wish I brought the local newspaper that I just bought into the diner with me. My stomach drops to the point that I do not feel hungry anymore. I want to get up and leave so I can sort this out on my own, but that would raise suspicion. I want to go to the truck and get the paper, but I do not dare. I force myself to choke down more soggy pancakes even though my appetite has vanished. I am staying pretty calm but there is pre-panic building up inside of me, wanting to blossom into full panic. I cannot deny that even with all the progress I have made on myself there are still limits to what strikes certain nerves. But, I am well aware that the smartest thing to do is act like I normally would, as if I am an ordinary innocent human being; even if it is not true.

"There's also a sketch of the guy in the paper, along with the article."

"Shit, look like anyone we know?"

"I don't think so. But almost everyone in town has seen it by now. It's just a matter of time before the bastard is caught."

I cannot finish this meal and get out of here fast enough. Nor can I tell if I am acting strange. I am dreading anyone coming over here and trying to interact with me before I can sort myself out. I have been so good lately at controlling my emotions that this is one thing I can forgive myself for getting stirred up about. It is and should be a major concern. Looking toward the tin devilish mystic I take a few inconspicuous deep breaths and figure that he is worth an ask. Silently, in my head, I ask it if the picture in the paper is me. The dime I shakily fished out of my pocket goes into the tin slot and the novelty card is pushed out:

YOU SHALL FIND OUT SOON ENOUGH.
WHEN THE TIME IS RIGHT,
YOU WILL KNOW WHAT TO DO.

Soon enough is not soon enough, in my mind. Eventually, I do finish my meal, pay and get out of there without hearing another word of the Avery case. I have not been around town enough the past few weeks to even know if she was found or not. For all I know she is still missing and this witness just remembers seeing someone. Or could it be that she was, in fact, found and now they are just getting all the final pieces of the crime to have a case and catch whoever did this? Too many variables to take any of this lightly.

When I get out of town I speed up the mountain and through the forest maze to the Elsewhere Church. This way, I can read the potentially damning newspaper in peace.

- Update On The Discovery Of Missing Woman's Body -
Saint Ox law enforcement discovered the mutilated body of
Avery Fletcher, 47, of Saint Ox early Monday morning in a
wooded area. Police do not wish to release further details of the
crime scene at this juncture. Over the last few days the
community has been encouraged to provide them with any
details at all that they may have regarding the crime. One
eyewitness came forward yesterday with new information, as
well as a detailed description of the suspect. A photo was drawn
by a Massachusetts forensic artist based on the description
provided by the witness.

To my relief, this sketch rendering has many of my
features wrong. The nose is a completely incorrect shape. Eyes
a bit too close together. Cheeks too round. This is still cause for
concern because they have come as close as I feared they might
in finding me. I have evolved so much since the Avery incident
and the missteps that I have taken may be coming back to haunt
me, one being the witness that I apparently had no idea of. I am
up against the hardest decision I have had to make since moving
here. Finding this church, the Church of Elsewhere, is the
greatest occurrence that has ever happened to me in my life up
to this point. It incited the whole whirlwind of events that led to
this ongoing betterment of myself. But, I'm afraid that the only
rational thing to do now is leave it behind. If I hang around the
Saint Ox area it will be just a matter of time before all the pieces
that the police put together usher them to me. It would be

foolish to think otherwise. Even with the somewhat inaccurate sketch, I still have no idea what else they know. They did not release much information regarding their investigation. This is standard practice to not let the public know everything they do because when they do finally take someone into custody they can cross reference these publicly unknown facts with the person who supposedly did it. Ask them things only the perpetrator would know. I will have to pack my things tonight and leave in the morning. There is no use lingering.

"When it's time to go, it's time to go," as Blue once told me.

Everything I own fits into the truck, as I have not accumulated much since moving in. The wicker chair stays. The pumpkins remain to rot themselves away as nature intended and regardless of whether I stay or not. The ones with heads in them stay out back where they are. The hands that once belonged to a very rude intrusive bald man, that now crudely stick to the podium, are chucked into the forest. The bodies I buried way back in the woods will remain there for a long time, maybe even forever. I remove the jars with Avery's eyes floating in formalin from the podium's repulsively mushy pumpkin. These are put under the floorboard where the LSD was hidden and discovered, while the LSD goes in the truck to take with me. Tools, cooking supplies, food, it all goes into the truck. The only thing left is my sleeping bag, which I will be using tonight to sleep in. I have decided that Monster will be left to fend for herself at the church. I do not know where I will end up or how long it will take me to get there. The possibility of coming back here exists, but it would have to be when the heat dies down from the Avery investigation. This could take years or longer. Even after police give up, the family and community in these kinds of affairs stay motivated. I let this thought leave my mind as there is no sense in dwelling on coming back anytime soon, or maybe ever.

The next morning I roll up my sleeping bag and eat two bananas while sitting in my wicker chair for the last time. Monster hovers around me. It is subtle, but I can tell she is acting differently. Ever since I packed up the church last night she seems to have a slightly distressed air about her. When the bananas are finished she gets the peels to pick at while I explain to her the situation.

"Listen, Monster. I made a mistake that we all have to deal with. When I first came to this place, before I even ran off with you from that farm, I met a lady, in passing, down there in town. I can't totally explain why, and of course your chicken brain doesn't understand any of this anyway, but just being around her got me so irrationally irritated. So much so that I followed her home and watched her for a few days in my abundant spare time. And one night I went into that home while she slept. At that time in my life I was unable to ignore these unsettling quirks and urges like I can now. I thought about taking a knife from the kitchen and painting her room red with blood. I thought about tying her up, gagging her mouth and then dragging her to the garage where I would leave her shut in with the car running. Someone would find her bound and yellow-eyed from the exhaust fumes; carbon monoxide poisoning. A ton of ideas swept through my head, but I just couldn't decide. So I went into her bedroom to watch her sleep and wait for a sign to tell me what the right course of action was. The urge built inside of me and I leapt onto the bed. This woke her up almost immediately, Monster. I stood up straight on the bed and she looked directly into my eyes. She was working up the energy to scream, I could tell. So I dropped down and covered her mouth. This turned into a stranglehold a second later and before I knew it she was unconscious. At the time, I was enthralled, excited, not nervous one bit. But looking back on the way I handled killing her makes my stomach churn. There were so many better ways to finish her off. I should not have left with her that night. Can I tell you something, Monster? She was the first person I have ever killed. I should have done it quick, right there in the room just to get it out of the way. Instead, I dragged her out of the house and around the corner, a block from where she lived, to the truck. This was entirely foolish on my part. Of course there is a witness, probably even more than one. We drove to the edge of town east of here, on the border of whatever the next town is, I have no idea because I have never gone back to this area again. There was tons and tons of forest here. I lugged her limp body way out in the middle of nowhere and woke her up. She began to scream at the top of her lungs. This made me so much more angry and intolerant of the woman. I slapped her hard and she stopped. She was disoriented. I wanted to get in her face and start yelling but I didn't. I pulled out my pocket knife and pressed it all the way into the side of her eye by the tear duct. Then I flicked the little knife with force and her eye popped right out. She tried to flee so I held her down by her neck on a large tree root bugling from the ground and popped out the other eye the same way. After that, I picked up her eyes and left. When I last saw her she was crying; not with her eyes for obvious reasons, but with pain filled yells. This was another mistake I made. It was my maiden murder and I didn't even stick around to see her die. There was not a doubt in my mind that she wouldn't survive long enough to find safety. She probably had a long bit of suffering and panicking before dying. But I should have finished her off or watched her die. I can never get a first chance again at this. That's it. And I'm ashamed."

I am surprised with how that chat with Monster went. When I started talking to her it was meant to be more of a goodbye, but I guess I had some unresolved insecurities to get off my chest. Issues I may have never talked about or admitted that I was ashamed of, even to myself. Closure, I suppose. The part of the tangent I stopped myself at is a good enough goodbye for me, and Monster probably could not care less. She continues to nervously stalk me in her suspicious manner this morning.

No need to keep dragging this out. I take one final look around the place before throwing a handful of oats and an apple to Monster. Then I shut the door to my snowy Elsewhere Church.

-3-

About halfway down the mountain towards Saint Ox something catches my eye in the passenger's side wing mirror. Could it actually be? Could Monster really have followed me all this way down the mountain? I stop the truck to see how this plays out. As the raptor-like creature gets closer it becomes apparent that, yes, Monster kicked her claws and fluttered her wings all this way along the mountain through the snow. She has an intense eagerness on getting herself to the truck. I am nearly in shock, or as close to shock as someone like me can get to feeling. She must have put it all together in her head when I was packing, the same way a dog knows when their owners are leaving for a long trip. I could tell she knew something was up, that was obvious, but for Monster to act on it is something I never would have credited her awareness with. I lean over and open the passenger door for her. I am skeptical she will know what to do, but she has ridden in a truck at least once before. Sure enough, she jumps in. First, to the panel on the dirty passenger floor mat, then hops up onto the seat. I reach over to close the door and we are back to getting off the mountain. Monster nestles up into herself and slumps right into a sleep. I can only imagine how exhausting that frantic trek down was for her.

I desperately need to fill the gas tank up and my only real option is to do it in Saint Ox. Ideally, I would be avoiding this town for the rest of my life, as of yesterday. But, here I am, at the pump nervously looking over my shoulder for a swat team to pin me down over some breakthrough in the case. This does not happen. The tank gets filled. I drive away. Monster stays sleeping. Goodbye, Saint Ox.

Talking to Monster is something that seems to be in the early stages of growing on me. We are just about out of Saint Ox when the uncertainty of the next location becomes more real.

"Okay, Monster, I have no idea where we're going or how far. Going east is out of the question because this is already nearly as far east as you can get. I came from the south and it doesn't make much sense to go back that way. North is an option but not the best one. There isn't that much left that way before hitting Canada and I don't want to risk a border crossing right now. West is the most logical direction. West it is."

PART FIVE

-1-

As we cross the border into New York on our westbound search
for something new, I end up unwittingly following a series of
familiar backroads. It started from my being lost in thought
when I took the subconsciously familiar series of exits and turns
that led to the upstate woodsy farmlands that I visited at the start
of my Elsewhere life. The old farm and farmhouse, out where I
still assume that no one ever really finds it, is barren from its
pumpkin patch and vineyard blossom as winter here has settled
in. The old couple who own the place are surely nestled up
inside, warming their brittle bones. A thin blanket of snow
covers the once gourd-plentiful field in back.

    I carry on along the dead-forested winding backroads
that I traveled once before; through the tiny communities of the
little farming townships that pop up. Everything is white and
brown from the snow covering all of the protruding dead trees. I
still find this just as visually appealing as when everything was
still mostly green. As I go further into these winter-dormant
wilds it feels like going backwards through time, closer and

closer to the colonial New England days. My heart skips a beat when the sign comes up:

Entering Bok

Unincorporated

Settled In 1791

The dead-looking arms and fingers of the trees that tunnel over the road give me a welcomed unsettling feeling, almost like the first time I stepped foot in the Elsewhere Church. At the same time, I have no idea why I am here. Canada will be approaching eventually if I stay following through in upstate New York, and I have already ruled out Canada as an option as not worth attempting. But still, I am keen to see more of this village that has captured my imagination for all this time.

I am not worried about being identified from the Eeka abduction like I am with the Avery one. I have complete confidence that no one was around on the secluded road where we met. Monster and I get out of the truck on this backroad so I can urinate and she can do whatever it is she needs to. For all I know she could take off running when I let her out. She does not. She jumps back into the truck when I open the door.

We now cross into the actual village, where all the Dutch colonial-style homes are spread out across the farmlands. The roads have all turned to dirt way back before I drove into the area, true to days long gone, before pavement ones. There are minimal amounts of snow on the ground here, with many patches of the green grass still visible all over. There is a brisk chill to the air, but the sun is shining bright. A man herds his ducks from a roughly conditioned barn into a fenced area in his field. His wife sits on the porch pouring hot tea for a group of ladies. They wear modest winter wool petticoats with shawls

196

and vintage double-breasted overcoats. They all hold books in their hands or laps, so I find it safe to assume that this is a book club. Another yard has three young children shoveling small piles of snow into one big pile with primitive wooden shovels. One older boy smooths the pile out into a sloping mass that is undoubtedly meant for sledding down. Their simple wood toboggans lay just beyond the white hill they have constructed. Cows and pigs walk in and out of barns to graze and take shelter. Another yard has a man pruning dead branches from trees while a different man tends a fire that burns them. The one burning the branches also looks to be taking trips to their small vineyard nearby and ripping off canes and spurs from the grapevines in neat rows held up by wiring. No other cars are out driving on these olden dirt roads. Not many cars to be seen around Bok at all, actually. The whole village has maybe twenty homes, or even less. Each spaced apart properly by their individual farmlands. At least half of the properties have a section for corn. The stalks on the rows of corn stand dormant and dusted with snow, while cut down to a height that reaches maybe just above my knee. As I continue down the beaten path that created this road, a man of around forty-five or fifty waves me down and moseys up to my truck. He wears clean black polyester trousers with black suspenders stretching over his cotton white shirt, and holds a black cotton coat under his arm.

"Hey, fella. I've been seeing you drive around," he says with no infliction.

I begin to get defensive in my head about this man and what his possible problems are with me. Then he continues.

"Just wanted to make sure you weren't lost or needed help. Are you? Do you?"

"No, just looking around. Visiting from Mississippi and taking backroads around New England. Ended up here," I say, trying to seem warm natured, but my words come out flat.

"Ah, wonderful scenery out here. We almost never get outsiders. Welcome. Care to come join us by the fire over there?" he points across the truck to a yard with a burning campfire.

I am caught way off guard by this. I believe following through with the invitation would be getting much too close for comfort considering I plucked one of their natives and killed her in violently cold blood. Regardless of this obvious bad idea, I accept. The immense dwelling I have done on this place since I first rolled through was too much to bear. I ended up back here for a reason, to examine Bok further, and before this man extended his invite it was turning out to just be another drive through town, like the first time.

"Sure, sounds good. Where should I park?"

He walked next to me while I pulled up onto the thinly snowy lawn.

"Wow! Is that a chicken you have riding with you?"

"Couldn't shake her, can you believe it? She just had to come with me."

"Everyone is going to absolutely love this. Come on."

Monster and I got out of the truck and followed the welcoming man. I am impressed with how she behaves like a well trained dog. She does her own thing but stays in close proximity to me. The man walks in front of us and chats as we head towards the campfire surrounded by a few others.

"My name is Luuk, by the way. These are my friends and my two daughters."

We all exchanged introductions. They have such peculiar names, but I meet so few people anymore that it is not too hard to remember them all. The girl with sandy blonde hair, who looks to be at the very end of her teens, is named Turinna. The brown haired one standing next to her, who looks very similar but a few years younger, is called Ahza. Both girls wear identical long dark green woolen petticoats with dark green capes wrapped around their upper halves and heads to match. Ahza and Turinna have genuinely kind smiles that you do not need to question, same as their father. The girls hold their hands out over the fire for warmth as they welcome me. Across the campfire from them is Wolrun, a man about the same age as Luuk, forty-five or fifty. His hair is average length and black, with a medium black beard to match. He is a good friend of Luuk's, as I assume everyone who lives in this small community are good friends. He wears a white cotton buttoned shirt and black trousers. The axe in his hand and the sweat pouring out of him tells me he was the one chopping, hauling and adding the wood for the fire. The last member of this group is called Servig. He is younger than the other two men but definitely older than me. I put him at mid-thirties. Servig has scruffy brown hair and a short untrimmed beard.

Wolrun asks, "So how did you get Monster to follow you like that?"

"Didn't have to do much. I actually never paid a whole lot of attention to her, besides when I was feeding her. Could be because she doesn't have a flock to bond with. She used to have one, but she was a loner around them. It's a mystery I guess."

A woman then comes up behind us with a tray of steaming mint tea for everyone and introduces herself as Maud, Luuk's wife.

"I see we caught a straggler in our little village. Hello there, I'm Maud."

The old me would be irritated with every conversation I have had with these people. Since living in the Elsewhere Church I have slowly been accepting the idea of being charmed. I am only just beginning to test the waters on this, but there may be something to embracing new feelings again. The bloodlust is still there within me, but for some reason, I do not feel it towards this crowd.

"Was just passing through and I was flagged down by your husband there. Nice little village you got here."

"Oh my, yes. This place is truly unlike anywhere else. You have to stay longer than just a pass through. You should come to the repast tonight," she says excitedly.

"I'm not sure if I know what repast is."

"A meal, dinner. A big feast," says Servig politely.

We talk as the fire is stoked and watched. They ask me questions about myself and I try to be as honest as possible, but I have no other choice than to lie about a great deal. These people seem smart and probably very intuitive. If I slip up at all they will be all over it.

-2-

The sun starts to set and the fire is just barely enough to keep us warm. When it gets dark enough I put Monster in the cab of my truck with the windows mostly rolled down. The rest of us stroll over behind the houses to a big field. Others from the community make their way into this area from all different directions as well. Two long wooden tables are situated in this field. It is now clear to me that the entire village will be attending dinner. When Maud invited me I thought it was going to be a meal with just the small group that was present at the fire.

When we are all seated an elderly, but still sharply able-bodied, man lights the many torches that surround the outdoor dining tables. A dozen young children then come out from one of the houses. Each of them hold a sizable plate or bowl of food that they set down on the two tables. A few of them run back and retrieve glass pitchers of water before they join the rest of the Bok community by taking a seat. The old man who lit the torches speaks up, addressing everyone with a booming presence in his voice, but at the same time, a bit rickety and wavering due to his advanced age.

"Hello again, everyone. It has been a productive week, as usual. All of the chores on our checklist have been completed and none of you should be surprised at this."

A few low affectionate chuckles come out from some of the people. The update about chores makes sense. Eeka had told me about how the elders discourage laziness and taught them to embrace work because slothful living causes unrest in the mind. So having a checklist each week adds up if that is their attitude.

"We have a guest here with us tonight, but I won't make it anymore awkward for him by putting him on the spot. Everyone be on your best behavior and show him how lovely it is here in Bok."

This is already super awkward, I am thinking. But, I am glad he did not make me get up and introduce myself or have everyone line up and greet me individually or anything of the sort. This is completely out of my usual comfort zone as it is. The thought of a whole group of people paying attention to me at once makes me quite unnerved. I am starting to miss my church more at this very moment as I dread that, eventually, there may be a moment when everyone wants to talk to me at once.

All of the torches around these tables do a surprisingly good job of keeping heat on us. The dishes of food are passed around to each of us so that everyone gets a chance to take whatever they want and add it to their plates. A large serving plate of roasted quail makes its way to me first and my mood shifts to excitement at the very sight. Food is now what is on my mind instead of potentially being the center of attention by a bunch of strangers. Bowls of diced and baked sweet potatoes float through. Slices of homemade rye bread, cornbread and sourdough bread each end up on my plate. Strips of steak. Steamed broccoli and carrots. Pickled eggs from chicken, quail and duck. Goat cheese. Arugula salad with beets. Baked buttery Brussels sprouts.

Everybody eats. I was almost certain that there would be some sort of ritual or religious chanting before anyone was allowed to eat. This place and these people give off so much religious fanatic vibes that it is almost even more unbelievable to me how normal they actually are, relative to what I expected. Some chattering happens here and there around the tables while we eat, like any typical family dinner. The conversation is brought my way a handful of times by those sitting close to me.

"How's the food?"

"It's great to have a guest here again. Been awhile."

"How long are you staying in the area?"

Nothing of great substance, more like jabber for trying to keep me feeling welcomed and engaged. I answer their questions sufficiently and go back to eating each time. They do the same.

I ask, "So, you people have a feast like this every week then?"

"Yes sir, every week. Unless we really slack on getting all of the work done around here. This community dinner is only part of our weekly ritual. A reward to ourselves. We take pride in staying busy and not letting our spirits rot in idleness. These are sentiments we try to pass down to our children as well. You saw how they brought us our meal. This is one of their chores. The adults cook the feast, but the children serve it, clear the tables and wash the dishes. The beginnings of proper work ethics and good habits," one woman explains to me.

A question emerges in my head. Finally, one I earnestly care to have answered.

"Just curious, why is the village called Bok?

"Ah, yes," a middle-aged man starts, "Bok is a Dutch word. It means 'billy goat', what a male goat is called."

He finishes that sentence and his head goes right back down, facing his food as he shovels a pickled chicken egg into his mouth. I was hoping for a bit more of a history lesson, but I suppose that can wait until after the meal. I failed to get the story of Bok from Eeka before I dispatched her.

The sun has long since set and it has been all the way dark out since around the time we started eating. I must admit that I like dining outside in the dark with just the dancing flames from a multitude of torches that keeps the warmth and the glowing light.

The tables are cleared by the same children who brought the meal out. When they return they carry pies with them. Apple, cherry, blueberry and peach pies. I opt for the cherry. During this course Maud, who sits two seats away, all but insists that I spend the night with them in their house.

"What kind of hosts would we be if we sent you on your way after dark?"

"I appreciate the offer, but it's probably best if I continue on my way tonight. It's really no problem. I can camp in my truck somewhere. I do it all the time."

"Ridiculous. You will stay with us tonight and figure out what happens next tomorrow. We have a spare room."

Now I definitely feel too close for comfort. My insecurities are flooding over me, and not even the ones pertaining to all of the things I do not want them to find out about. I have a difficult time in general being around people this long. I live very deliberately disconnected from others because I do not know how to handle it, except for brief spells at a time. I hate being forced to admit these things to myself, about myself. Every instinct inspires me to run away.

"How could I argue with that? I guess I'm staying."

"Great! After the weekly ritual is over we will show you to your room."

"Good choice on staying. Going to be cold tonight around these parts," Luuk voices to me from the other end of the table.

-3-

The tables have been totally cleared. Everybody stands up at their own pace and half of them grab hold of a torch. Maud and Luuk's daughter Ahza nudges me to take one also.

"It's okay. Here, take this one. Helping light the path, this can be your contribution."

All the village of Bok now walks out across the field, further away from the houses. Suddenly, Monster runs up to the

side of me. She must have jumped out of one of the truck
windows. I acknowledge her so that everyone knows she is not
some rogue chicken from their farm. Nobody seems to pay
much mind about it and even seem fairly charmed that Monster
follows close behind my step. Pretty soon the field ends and
turns into forest.

We cross the dormant forests threshold and come upon
a significant structure. A large log cabin building. It looks like it
extends back a good way, so I can imagine everyone fitting
inside without much discomfort. The wood trim around the
entrance is elaborately carved in flowery designs. I can barely
wrap my head around how anyone could create such intricate
carvings this way. In between the flowery shapes are animals
and animal features like teeth and horns. This trim that borders
the huge doorway is only the start. On the outside logs that
structure the walls, and the entire building itself, are carved
symbols and shapes that resemble hieroglyphs or some kind of
alphabet that I have never seen before. With a torch in my hand
I stand surrounded by an inviting community with depths I am
beginning to realize I know nothing about. The forest is dead
and silent. The only thing I can hear right now is the pops and
cracks of the torch flames. Something needs to happen soon or I
might implode.

The senior man, who spoke to the town before the feast,
joins another elderly man in front of the entrance to the great
cabin. They speak to the torch-lit mob of Bok in turns.

"The feast was exquisite, as usual, everybody."

"Yes, another marvelous banquet this week. Our guest
is probably wondering what exactly is happening right now.
Hopefully we haven't scared him off."

"Him and his feathery companion there."

"Right, him and Monster. We trust they are comfortable enough to join us in our weekly ceremony. Would you do us the honor?" one of them directed at me.

Every initial instinct I have, again, says to get out of there quickly. As someone who does not behave normal, I can recognize that this is not normal behavior. Everyone turns their attention to me. I weigh my options of trying to escape or telling myself that everything is fine, how it should be, and to just go with it.

"Well, I'm already here with you all. Might as well keep on being here."

This statement of accepting another one of their invitations causes a kindly laugh from a few in the crowd. Monster scratches around a bit, but mostly just stands alert as this is all happening.

"Super. Well then, let's head inside the ritual hall. Ernst is waiting for us."

We all file into this cabin, one and two at a time. Most of the torches are left stuck in the ground outside. I am somewhere in the middle of the crowd by the time everybody is inside. The walls have iron sconces with lit candles on them. There are also two big candelabras made from deer antlers on either side of the entrance, adorned with candles holding steady flames to testify to the calmness of the room now. On one side of the room there is a large wooden trunk that almost looks like a treasure chest. Each person lined up to take a mask from the big box. I was coaxed up to the front to get in on the mask choosing before most of the others. When I stood before the container of masks I mention to one of the men, who was around my age, that I have the perfect mask of my own in my truck and if they had told me about this I could have grabbed it beforehand. With that information he whispers to one of the children something that had probably been along the lines of encouragement to go retrieve it for me. The man asks where in the truck it is and I tell him it should be on the passenger side floor mat. I vividly recall throwing it there as I was packing up the truck before leaving the Elsewhere Church. If it were somewhere in the truck bed then I would have to deny any rummaging. It would be too risky of me to potentially let them discover the ether mask or bloody razor wire or journal or anything else I cannot think of right now. The front area is safe as can be for me. The young boy bolts through the crowd with haste and is back from my truck to the cabin, tengu mask in hand, in just about the time that everyone has gotten a mask for themselves.

The people wear these masks made from solid material of hard woods and metals. Some of these just cover the eyes and nose while others veil the entire face. Carved wood or forged metal to look like animals. Wolf, bull, ram, bird and elk are all among them. Also, humanoid types are present with accentuated features; Plague doctors with long beaks, demons, jesters with soundless dangling bells, nameless forest creatures, even a few similar to my tengu mask with the long noses and honed teeth. They are all mostly dark, burnt and rusted, but somehow natural looking colors like deep crimson red, black, dark gold, copper, shady silver, gloomy forest green and the occasional ivory white. Most of the metal ones have silver, red or black designs outlined over parts of their sculpted faces. Horns or antlers or feathers protrude from many of these disguises. Some don a friendly and noble look. Others are angered and wicked. This masquerade has a heightened hellish elegance now that we all stand in the dimly lit log cabin wearing our masks. I am actively forcing myself to withdraw from asking anything at all. The atmosphere is too enigmatic to interrupt with any silly question that only I would need answering. I have accepted that this will be a mystifying experience no matter what happens. The way I figure it is that this will either turn sexual, violent or religious. Possibly all three, but it is totally out of my hands now. I can only stand, wait and hope that barbarous things are not destined to be inflicted on me.

A canvas sheet in back, the same color of the low lit walls, is drawn away to the side. Up until now, I thought this was an actual wall and we were standing in the full stretch of the building. It turns out, behind the canvas, the room extends another third of the way. A thick wooden fence makes a barrier between our room and the newly presented one that stands up to my chest. In this enclosure stands an abundantly longhaired goat. He is all black except for some white in his beard and down his cheeks. The horns on this beast are impressive. They start by going straight up above the head just a bit and then wing straight outward at both sides to the length of my outstretched arms. The woman I am standing next to leans over and tells me that this is Ernst, and that he is a Dutch Landrace breed with a rare wild Irish goat mixed in, along with some kind of ancient breed from the Middle East. Ernst stands stoic in his pen surrounded by a substantial bed of hay. It could be because I am standing here with a town of masked onlookers in a ritualistic fashion, but Ernst appears to be very self aware. To the point that whatever is about to happen, he is guiding it. One of the older gentlemen pipes up again in his refined silvery metal skull-like mask with thin red tracings around it.

"By now our guest is definitely wondering what is happening and what he should be doing. Before we start, I think it's fair to give him a brief history and explanation. Does this sound okay to you all?"

Many voices spoke up in agreement and were rather enthused by the idea of hearing their story again, or perhaps because they get to share it with a stranger. It occurs to me that they probably do not often share this world of theirs with many others. Stories and lives like this, from what I have seen so far, would spread around like wildfire and end up being common knowledge. I am starting to think that they chose me in some way.

"Wonderful. Firstly, I would like to mention that this is Ernst," he says, while motioning behind himself to the large shaggy goat.

"Ernst and his ancestors have been with Bok for many generations. Since the beginning of us, really. The village of Bok can be traced all the way back to the New Netherland settlement of what was a Dutch province in the early sixteen-hundreds here. At this time, the only native goats, to what is now North America, were mountain goats. Mountain goats were only native to the Pacific Northwest region of North America and on into the Yukon Territory. So, when our descendants brought them over it was the first introduction of goats to this area of upstate New York. The Dutch Landrace breeds that were imported here served all sorts of useful functions for our colonist ancestors. Milk, leather, meat, warm blankets from their hides and fur. They also did groundskeeping by keeping the grass and weeds trim from grazing. As with most colonist and native peoples relations, these two groups often clashed. Onslaughts were occasionally made by each side against the other. The most historic attack made, in the history of Bok's account, was an ambush one night by the indigenous warriors of the settled area. The natives raided Bok by torching crops and killing the livestock. A counterstrike, that goes back and forth, in a long list of attacks from both parties. By the time the assault ended, all of the goats had perished. Except one. A billy goat they called Ernst. This buck was their pride and joy for weeks afterwards. Every single animal had died during the attack except for him. In addition to all the dead goats, there were chickens, pigs, dogs, some cows and horses. Ernst, being a male goat, did not help them with getting milk, which was their main resource regarding goats. But he became a symbol of hope. You see, the night everything was burned and killed, as they were putting out the fires in a frenzy after the natives left, Ernst spoke to them. Flames surrounded them in every direction and he emerged on the main path between the river where they gathered extinguishing water and their village that was aflame."

"He told them, 'Believe in the flame. Give thanks and respect to it tonight as you put it to death. Because this element is crucial to your survival as well as potential demise. Give praise to the natives for giving you this opportunity to hear me speak. Hail them for the land they cherished, that you now inhabit. Do not hate destruction as you do not hate creation. If you, every single one of you, agree to embrace what I have to teach then I will help you extinguish this fire.' And then Ernst paused."

I stood there masked and in awe. This is the exact kind of history I was hoping to hear tonight. I am completely lost for a moment in this and forgot about all the mysteriousness surrounding my current affairs. Even the nervousness of not getting far and fast enough away from the Avery situation has totally dissolved for the moment. I am just hanging on the old man's words, ready for the next ones to come out.

"The people all agreed. They were in too much shock of what they just experienced to not give in. So the goat went down to the river as the people scattered once more; some filling up buckets of water, some throwing water on the fire and

everywhere in between. When Ernst got to the river he had
eleven buckets. Five on each long horn and one in his mouth.
He carried this load up to the burning homes and the people
grabbed the buckets from him. He waited to see what their
reaction to this act was. Would they renounce his help, thinking
that because he could talk he had special fire dousing powers
instead of just basic bucket carrying abilities? Would they praise
him for whatever assistance he could contribute? He was
looking to make sure their commitment to him and their
agreement was authentic. When Ernst heard them vocally
thanking the fire as they doused it out slowly he knew they were
sincere in the bargain. With that, he began to jump up and down
in front of everyone. He kicked and stomped and bleated lowly
while thrashing his head in some kind of frantic dance. Before
he finished his gambols the skies opened up and cracked a
roaring thunder louder than any of them have ever heard. The
rains fell down like an enormous ocean wave and smothered the
fire within seconds. From there on forward they began their
traditions and rituals based around the sentiments that Ernst had
to teach them. The ideals of this revolve around destruction and
creation, like in the agreement speech Ernst gave to the
townspeople as Bok burned. He also taught them the importance
of solitude and solidarity, much like you may have picked up on
here tonight. Do you have any thoughts on this or questions?"
he directed at me.

I surely had many thoughts and questions after this
story. I could not get them out of my head on the spot like that,
with him and everyone waiting.

"So, the goat from hundreds of years ago when Bok was
settled is the same goat that is right behind you?"

This was the first and foremost thing on my mind.

"Ah, I should have continued further. No, this is not the same goat. The Ernst from way back then lived a normal length life and died much the same as any other goat does. Though, he was made very comfortable after that gifted rainstorm he brought to save the homes from burning to the ground. The Ernst you see now is a direct descendant, though. His bloodline is very well preserved. He is royalty now, on a few different levels. Not only is Ernst of a noble bloodline to us here in Bok, for his mystical otherworldly mysteriousness he has shown us, but because of who he was then bred with to keep his line continuing. Only weeks after that historic night, a group of Spanish colonists made their way from their originating settlement on the southwestern part of North America to here in the New Netherland province. With them, they brought their own goats. A few, in particular, were believed to be descendants of the original goats ever to exist upon the earth; the Adam and Eve of goats, if you will. They went on a secret crusade to retrieve these goats from the Fertile Crescent in the region of what is now modern day Syria. The milk from these descendants is supposed to be celestially powerful. It is meant to cure illness, provide divine health and connect you with ethereal powers. There was no way of knowing if it was true, until that original Ernst himself spoke to them on the matter and confirmed the greatness of the Spaniards herd. The village pulled together a massive amount of what resources they had left in order to purchase a female goat of this elite lineage from them. Which they did and the Spaniard travelers carried on wherever they were going. The ancestry of Ernst here has been one of nobility and heightened capability ever since."

I am silent after this explanation. The old masked man can tell I am through with questions for now. He reaches into a bucket beside him and pulls out a carrot that he then feeds to

Ernst. Now, in my mind, he has so much more presence to him. The man reaches again into the bucket to pull out a handful of pellet feed and throws it into the pen. At the sound and sight of this Monster takes off, darting towards the worshipped billy goat cage. My stomach sinks because I can only imagine that there are repercussions for this sort of thing. She hops up into the enclosure and pecks wildly around at the feed on the ground. Every last one of the persons inside the log goat sanctum sees this.

If I was unsure about them harming me or not before, I can certainly see a reason for it now. Dead silence all around, while an encompassing attention is paid to what is happening with Monster. Unexpectedly, an adoring laugh comes out from someone. This must be contagious because many others make the same sound. Relief washes over me and I can breathe again. I can see faint smiles on the faces of those with masks not covering their mouths. Ernst pays no mind to the chicken scratching and pecking around below him. The old man throws a few more handfuls of feed in her direction. Then he pulls a rope which draws up a door on the back wall of the goat enclosure. It leads to an unfenced outdoor area for Ernst to graze. Me, in my long-nosed blue tengu demon mask, and the others in their assorted beastly disguises, all walk through the gate of the pen and out the lifted opening, following behind Ernst.

It is dark, but the moon and few torches we have with us give just enough light to see around this clearing in the woods. Hay lightly coats the grass where we are and two water troughs are set by the cabin. Where the forest circles us and starts again there are three little barns spaced apart evenly. Other goats and livestock must be put up inside for the night. In the center of this glade are some hay bales in a pile with long logs crisscrossing below and on top of them. Two of the young torch holders walk over to the pyre and set it ablaze. The people of Bok began a chant while looking at the fire.

"We thank the flames and their destruction. We call on the goat to ease the blaze," they repeated over and over.

After about a minute of this the goat started dancing wildly. Bucking, kicking, jumping, bleating, thrashing, head shaking and spinning around fast enough that you could imagine his long outstretched horns cutting right through anything that got close enough. The clouds covered the moon and dimmed the scene so that it was now only illuminated by fire light. Raindrops started to fall upon us, slowly at first. Then a crash of lightning brought on torrential rainfall. The fire that burned ferociously before us was defeated. Not even smoke or smoldering coals managed to survive a few seconds of the downpour. Monster stood in the doorway of the cabin, watching the whole spectacle from this dry shelter. The rain tapers off over the next few minutes and we are all soaked. Ernst moseys his way back into the cabin pen and Monster sprints over to me before the door is lowered back down. The last thing I see of Ernst before this is him lying down in a comfortable curled up position on a bed of hay.

The masks were collected by the children and everyone went back to their homes. There were no more stories or explanations by anyone in the village before making for their houses. Just simple goodnights and see you tomorrows. I walked to my truck to drop the mask off and get a change of clothes and toothbrush before taking on the assignment I agreed to; the assignment of spending the night with the family I just met and partook in a cultish routine with. A woman from a

neighboring farmhouse offers to house Monster in one of her
small coops with five other chickens. Monster does not care
much to socialize with the others, but she accepts the coop to
sleep in and the others do not seem bothered by her. She
collapses in a nesting box and falls right to sleep.

-4-

Luuk and Maud greeted me at the door and their two daughters,
Turinna and Ahza, stood watching from the staircase. The inside
of their home was much like the outside, in the sense that it
feels like from a time long ago. In front of me, from the
doorway, was a hallway leading straight through to a living
room. On the right side of this hallway was the staircase that
went up and to the left. I was surrounded by a deep, dark stained
eastern pine wood interior. Everything from the floors to the
walls were made of this rustic wood. I can make out a grand
fireplace, probably made of granite, in the living room. This
living room is decorated by furniture made of wood that still has
bark on it with leather and fur cushioning. The home is a
confirmed authentic farmhouse without me having to see the
rest of it.

The family does not offer to give me the grand tour at
this late hour. Instead, they escort me upstairs and show me to
my room for the night. It is a typical girl's room with flowing,
cream white bedding and curtains. Flowery feminine pictures
hang on the walls of gardens and elegant women. There is a
vanity table, made of that same dark pine as the rest of the
house, with a mirror and pictures wedged in around the frame.

I drop my bags and go to the washroom to take a shower; a suggestion to me by the family who have now all gone to their beds. This is the first time since I drove up to New England from Mississippi that I have used a home shower. The handful of times I took myself to bathe had always been at the recreation center in Saint Ox. I made it a quick rinse as I did not want to keep my hosts and because the sooner I go to sleep the earlier I might wake up to leave here.

I do feel a sense of comfort with these people, but also a great sense of awkwardness as I feel around everyone and anyone at all, especially when I have spent this amount of time with them. I poke around the room before settling in to bed. The dressers have some clothing, most likely the excess articles from Turinna and Ahza. Little trinkets and modest jewelry are spread out on top of the dresser and vanity table. The pictures pushed into the sides of the mirror frame show Luuk and Maud at a younger age, one of either Ahza or Turinna as a baby in a bassinet, one of a little girl petting a horse. The last few pierce me with shock. They are all of Eeka. Young Eeka holding hands with Maud. Eeka with Ahza and Turinna and a few other girls. Eeka smelling flowers in a huge garden. I was feeling tired a moment ago, but now some adrenaline has kicked in. This is Eeka's family. Her mom and dad. Her two sisters. Her yard, her wash room, her home. This room is not just a spare room, it is Eeka's. Was Eeka's. I am about to sleep in the bed of a girl I murdered. Invited and welcomed. There is something exciting about this. I feel like I was nearly turning a corner with a fading bloodthirstiness, but this has been another sign that I was on the right track all along. The consequence of killing an innocent person has been to reward me with hospitality from the people she was viciously plucked from. I should not lose sight of this. Controlling my agitation and awkward impulses has led me to accept their hospitality and gave me the fulfilling experience of seeing how this village works. Also, the chance to be a part of an actual effective ritual.

As I lay in Eeka's bed I allow all sorts of thoughts to pass through my head. I spend a good while thinking about Ernst and the history of Bok. At some point, I would like a more in depth history lesson on the matter.

I think about Eeka, briefly. I think about the Elsewhere Church, briefly. I think about what it would take for me to spend more time here. It seems so crazy that I am actually entertaining a thought in being part of a community, of choosing to be around people.

-5-

I am standing in a field, surrounded by forest. It is nighttime and extremely dark out, but somehow, I am much more aware of my surroundings than I rightfully should be. I can see the sliver of a moon in the black sky. Eeka walks up beside me, looking the way she did the day I met her; a long dark blue and white dress with full length sleeves. She turns her head to me and whips her light brown hair behind her. The smirk she displays tells me nothing. She looks into my eyes deeply with her chestnut brown ones and does not say a word as she begins to walk. I already know she wants me to follow her without having to ask. We walk to the woods where we come upon a large cabin. Everything feels fine as I go with the flow and question nothing. We enter the cabin where a candlelit room awaits us. In the back of this room sits a large, shaggy black goat with great

*big horns and a white beard. We are face to face with the goat
now. He stands up on his two hind hooves. He looks down at me
and the room starts to get brighter. I turn around to see that the
candles along the walls have turned to flames that burn the
wood and spread across it. Eeka is gone and the flames grow
bigger, engulfing the room. I turn my attentive stare back to the
goat who still continues to gaze at me. Way up above him are
three round faces formed from the dark orange inferno that I
recognize immediately. They, too, leer at me.*

The next morning we, the family and I, gather in front
of the old granite fireplace in the living room. We drink coffee
and juice while warming up. I have firmly decided not to bring
up Eeka from fear I will say the wrong thing and possibly give
myself away. Instead, and without showing awe in the
phenomenon I witnessed last night in the woods behind the log
cabin, I ask about the rituals that they perform.

"I was told you all do a different ritual every week?"

"Yes, we make sure to keep our weekly ceremonies on
rotation so things don't get boring."

"It was quite a show. I'm curious about what other
kinds of ceremonies you do at these weekly events."

"Sometimes we dance. Other times we pray. Most of the
time Ernst gifts us with a display and some sort of experience,
like the one you saw last night. On very rare occasions there is a
sacrifice."

I had a delayed reaction to this last part, so the
statement that Luuk just made hung with silence for a moment
afterwards.

"So you choose an animal from the livestock and bring
it out to be killed as an offering to Ernst?"

"Sometimes an animal and sometimes one of our villagers."

"I see," was all I could muster.

The family could see that I was reaching for words to come up with to ask more about how that all works. Instead of letting me struggle over how to inquire further, Maud chimes in.

"It's not what you may be thinking. We don't drag one of our own out into a field against their will and chop their head off."

"Ah, so it's more of a performance than an actual sacrifice?"

"Oh no, we do take someone out to the field and decapitate them. But we do not do this against anyone's will. It's all done strictly by sincere volunteering. We don't, in any way, encourage or push our kin to enlist for such a gesture. Nor do we delude them by suggesting that they will get some great reward in the afterlife. We simply have no way of knowing this," Maud explains.

Luuk chimes in while the girls listen and brush each other's hair.

"The sacrifices are so few and far between. When it does happen, it is usually from someone who is deathly ill or, in a few cases, has incurable depression. There have also been a few times where there seemed to be no real outside reason to why the person volunteered. This is the case with Eeka, our daughter."

I am so nervous about tripping over my words if I try to speak. But, if I do not say anything it could seem even more suspicious.

"Your daughter was sacrificed? How interesting," I say, being sure not to give the usual sorry for your loss regurgitation that everyone says when someone dies.

This, as far as I know in their minds, was a supported offering to the community and might not warrant condolence.

A mournful essence overtook the room and Ahza spoke up in a somber tone.

"My sister disappeared a few months ago."

"Yes, our daughter was a committed individual to our community. We were quite surprised when she submitted herself for sacrifice. But, a few days before she was to be offered up she vanished."

"That's terrible. Any idea where she went or what could have happened?" I say, trying to suggest she may have run away or at least could be out in the world, alive, somewhere.

"It would be very uncharacteristic of her to run off. Our kind have settlements in New Mexico and Oregon, as well, but she loved her life and the community here in this one. The truth about what happened to her will come to light someday. Don't you agree?"

This question was quite unsettling at first because it was firmly directed at me and in no way rhetorical. With deep stares coming from each family member, they wanted an answer. My initial inner feelings at this moment are nothing but nervous. Nothing else at all, really. I do not feel guilt about taking Eeka. If I were to separate from the unsettled nerves I feel, due to her family's direct proximity to me, then I would have to say I could identify a sense of fulfillment. With everyone I have harmed in my life, I have never gotten the chance to be this close to the other people it directly affects afterwards. I do not care much about their feelings. Are they distraught for their missing daughter? Are they coping and moving on? Do they lose sleep and stay distracted throughout their days since she disappeared? The truth is still, I do not care. My realized pleasure in being around them now does not come from seeing them suffer or not. It has nothing to even do with me wanting these people to suffer or not suffer, because it does not matter to me. I simply take a spark of gratification in being able to observe what happens to a family when one of their kin is taken. Now, I shrug off the tension to welcome my true sentiments. Sit back and watch everything unfold organically like they were animals at the zoo, minus the cages.

One thing that is keeping me in awe is the fact that Eeka was going to sacrifice herself. I reflect on this for a second and consider what her grounds for this choice were. If I had pressed her about her life here would she have told me? She had plenty of opportunities to share all kinds of things that I have now witnessed about her beloved Bok. However, Eeka only dispensed the bare minimum of intriguing information that she possibly could. Perhaps, also, I should be feeling some sort of disempowerment in knowing the fact that she was destined, by her own choice, to be killed soon anyway. Maybe best not to think of it that way; better to accept that, yes, she had already made the decision to die on her own terms, but I was still able to take that choice away and destroy her on my own terms.

I have paused long enough since their inquisition about whether or not the truth will come out. Maybe a bit too long.

"I think you will see your daughter again someday," I announce with a forced reassuring half-smile.

"Thank you for saying that. We think so too. And thank you for being here. Luuk and I had a talk last night and we were hoping you would stay with us a little longer, in our spare room. We're certain that this is what Eeka wants too. She would be absolutely insisting on it if she were here right now. There's still a lot more we'd like to show you around Bok. And I'm certain there are some things you could show us."

Eeka's mother was right. I feel drawn to this place and their rituals. A curiosity that began months ago, when passing through that country road, tunneled by trees, upon that fundamental first meeting with Eeka. There definitely are some things I could show them, too. I am getting flashes of that dream I had, the one where I saw Eeka in the drab garden. She told me to follow her. Always follow what she says. As hard as it is to find the meanings in my recent dreams, I can attribute what she said there to this moment now. I am following her trail back to her origins. Is this reaching too much? Do our dreams really have messages behind them when they are happening? Or is it up to us to interpret their messages how we see fit, in a way that suits us?

My goal yesterday was to get as far away from New England as possible. Today, I am beginning to have second thoughts.

A new story is about to begin for me.

EPILOGUE

Spring is just around the corner and my A-frame cabin is nearly complete. The weather is consistently above freezing and the denizens of Bok have helped me build this modest home in the middle of their forest, per my stated desire to be more remote. I have helped Eeka's family with many duties and drudgeries throughout winter in exchange for room and board. The village has accepted me as one of their own and, while I still have the urge to carry on my work of ending lives, I have no desire to act upon this with anyone else from Bok. Monster mostly stays at the neighboring farm that took her in on the first night we arrived. She runs out whenever I am around to come join me in whatever job I am doing that day, but her home has been with the neighbors. I figure when I have my own home and garden all set up she can come stay with me if she chooses.

The weekly rituals have opened me up to the acceptance of a community, one that suits me with only minimal reluctance on my part, at least. We have seeds started indoors at Eeka's former home to plant outside in the garden when it warms up a bit more. Tomatoes, watermelon, okra, peppers, broccoli, lettuce, eggplant, cabbage and, of course, pumpkin. Many, many pumpkin seedlings. When the pumpkins are ready to be picked later in the year I will begin my work again, in full force. The three carved companions and myself, their haunted captain and creator.

In all honesty, I will probably start the depravity before the pumpkins are ready. Treading very lightly around Bok when doing so is going to be crucial and difficult. I am hoping there may be some kind of deal to work out with Ernst on the matter of me killing in his forest, but I have no idea how to go about presenting this quite yet.

Dreams of Zipper, Blue and Ghost have halted completely, for now. This will no doubt change when pumpkin season begins.

There have been a few times that I have seen The Ocean come to me while I sleep, though. I am always on that massive antiquated wooden war ship. It is consistently that grey ominous darkness of night. I will walk from end to end of the ship while looking out at the endless sea of small blue pumpkins and their faces. Sometimes I walk down into the other chambers of the vessel and discover new rooms that I have not seen before. A room with rows of holding cells for prisoners, the brig. Storage closets with clothes or weaponry or crates filled with something I cannot imagine. The large kitchen room, that a crudely carved sign calls the galley, and the mess hall that is attached to it. Sleeping quarters with bunk beds padded by loose straw. Once, I climbed up the main mast to the crow's nest, hoping to get a better vantage point to possibly see land in some direction. It was futile, The Ocean went on forever. I did make the discovery of Eeka's name roughly etched into the wood up there, though. I have not seen Eeka since the last time I saw the others. The only difference with her is that I can feel her presence, like she is around me, waiting for a moment to reveal herself once again.

Overall, most of my time in these nautical dreams that I occasionally return to is spent either on the upper deck or in the captain's chamber. These areas seem to be the most comforting for me during those sleeping hallucinations that, truthfully, sometimes feel lucid. The strangest thing about it all is when I look into the cloudy desilvering mirror hanging on the wall in the captain's chamber. The face that looks back at me is the demon face of the captain, the one I spoke with the first time I dreamed this up; the face of that mask I stole from the Turkish fortune teller at that Halloween festival in Connecticut, the same one that I wear to the rituals here in Bok. Sharp-toothed, long-nosed, piercing devious eyes that are indistinguishable from happy or angry and navy blue in color. This is what I have become in my slumbering shadow world.

I dwell on this thought from time to time. The tengu demon image being me; what I have evolved into. I believe that this metamorphosis can be traced back to Halloween. Stalking those victims in that Connecticut graveyard, this was the moment I crossed the threshold into a proper genesis of the beast I was meant to become someday. A glimpse of the truly artful depravity that I hope to advance on. Eeka was and is the wonderful overture for which this growth could not have happened without.

My Elsewhere Church will be a second home for me, always. I hope to get back there to spend another extended barbarous vacation in the Berkshires. This will take, at best, a few years to be able to stay there comfortably. I think that the heat from Avery will surely be lingering around those parts for some time. This is fine with me for now since I have begun a life in Bok. It almost seems too perfect that the village preaches solitude as one of their main beliefs. I figure that this is why they allowed me my cabin to be way out in the forest. With the agreement of contributing to the village duties, of course.

In times like this I am thankful that I have a mind capable of critical thinking. The mentality that enables me to leave my mental comfort zone in order to relocate myself into the unknown and find a place in the world. I consider people I grew up with from back home, or even people that I have met throughout my life, who have never once left the area they were born into. There is a sense of unresolved misery in some of them that they may never recognize. It is not that improbable to think that maybe not everyone is born into the exact place they were meant to live forever. Some of us need to go out and discover where we are meant to be. Those who are meant for this, but never figure it out, end up drenched in despair without ever knowing the reason why. I wonder what the odds are that someone starts out, from day one, in the place where they are most likely to thrive?

Every time I look at Eeka's parents I can picture the beautiful moment that my knife went through her head, forcefully, while a second before she was manically laughing. Crazed and drugged and scared out of her mind.

The one thing that worries me and crosses my mind daily is that someone will discover and read my journal. Since I have been staying with Eeka's family, in her room no less, there is not much privacy to be had. Many times when I was out working around the village the family had gone into the room for all different reasons; retrieve a jewelry piece, a garment, collect my laundry, vacuumed the floor or simply just to look at the many pictures that Eeka had decorated her room with. It is not my place to insist on privacy while I am a guest in their home. The truck is also not an option because I semi-regularly let someone use it. There are only a few vehicles in Bok, and occasionally they are all in use or broken down. Anything else in my truck that may seem suspicious could be explained away if discovered. I already have excuses lined up for the questionable items, but the journal would be utterly damning. The only exception to what they could probably stomach reading is all of my long-winded explanations where I carry on about food or repairing the church and things like that. Regardless, without privacy or any proper place to hide the journal, and without having to throw out my personal chronicles, I must make sure no one reads my writings. This would expose me as the reason why Eeka had disappeared, and in such a torturously gruesome manner; and all of the other things I have done, along with my wild dreams and crazed thoughts. I have no idea how Bok would handle a discovery of information like that.

After much internal toiling I have decided to take a trip back to the Elsewhere Church and hide my journal there. Deep down in the ground where no one would ever find it except me, even if the church itself is discovered. It makes the most sense for this particular journal to live there anyway. And when my cabin in the Bok forest is built I can rest easy and start an entirely new journal with my own space to figure out an appropriate spot for it to be hidden.

The plan for Saint Ox and Elsewhere is also to be inconspicuous and feel out what the Avery situation is like while passing through. I will spend the night at the church and head right back to Bok.

I arrive at the Elsewhere Church a few hours before the sun begins to set. This gives me plenty of time to dig an exceedingly deep hole in the woods beyond the church. Ravens have taken over the inside and have helped themselves to the rotting pumpkins. This is fine with me for now as I am only here to dig, sleep and then leave.

Monster has joined me on the road trip. The first thing she does when we get there is run to her old nest under the front pew and lay an egg. I will be far too busy to worry about collecting and eating it, so I figure it belongs to the ravens now.

My suspicions about the Avery predicament were confirmed. It has been months since her mutilated body was found and there are still fresh posters of my wrongly sketched face stapled on most of the telephone poles. The radio played a segment about who Avery was and how the town needs to continue looking for answers. I have the information I came for now and it is apparent that I need to stick to my plan and get out of here as fast as possible tomorrow morning.

I have now gone through many layers of earth to a depth around half of my own height. In this time, I am able to contemplate the marrow of my pilgrimage from this past autumn and winter. I thought I was going to come to some sort of conclusion with all these killings. Some kind of realization about myself and a newfound way to enhance my life. And this is true, in some respects. But honestly, I think I just like killing people. That is the bottom line. I have eliminated the angst I used to feel towards my victims. This allows me to fully enjoy my craft without drowning in rage and succumbing to temper; all while keeping the passion that goes hand in hand with it. This is a simple realization, but a significantly important one. Everything that has happened here is only the beginning for me.

Before I place the journal into its crypt, made of three tightly wrapped garbage bags and one wooden box, I take a seat above the grave and thumb through my writings while catching my breath.

I reread a few of my vicious doings and some of my dream entries. These are all things that I am glad to have written down and looking forward to someday having the chance to seriously reflect back on. I can see that the early entries are less streamlined or pronounced than my later, more recent ones. Those older jottings have a much higher sense of blatant bitterness in their cadence. The words in those first pages make me cringe at the person I was; and with such lengthy over-explanations to make it worse. The further I go through the pages of my time in New England, so far, the wording becomes more coherently refined and structured. A sobered pulse within its lifeblood emerges eventually and only gets better. I truly hope to continue writing this way in another journal to improve my technique.

There are already many parts of my recent dreams that I have forgotten about. As I scan them over, the meanings behind them are comfortingly ambiguous. But I still read into the fact that they did actually mean something. Dreams are compelling in this way; they demand a search for interpretation. Dreams and nightmares surely cannot just be the flooding of dopamine and neurotransmissions. An exact mixing of neurochemicals might be an acceptable way in explaining the catalyst for dreams, but how can it explain their actual meanings, their reason? I realize that my three pumpkin visitors have given me much to dwell on the more I flip through these pages. And all of the frequent abrupt moments that cut away, only to immediately put me back to where I was, will always baffle me. Perhaps these are simply to keep you on your toes and to make one stay alert and dreaming. I could speculate forever with all sorts of different perspectives on this, but I really do not have the time right now.

Shocking mental panic strikes me as I read the short entry in the very last page. It is not my handwriting. Someone else has written here. Violated my book of personal thoughts and histories. I feel defiled. I wish I had seen this sooner. It has been a while since even opening this journal of mine, but someone other than myself has definitely found their way inside of it. This was clearly someone from Bok. But which one? Probably more than one. Who would have had the chance without me noticing? There were likely many chances, if I am to be honest.

We didn't have to read this journal. Ernst already told us everything you've done ages ago. Eeka is needed here and we would like to speak with her.

-Bok

They know, and it appears that they have known, of the things I have done. But if they really do know everything then how could they expect to speak with Eeka again? And why would they write it down for me to find instead of plainly confronting me? I find it just about impossible to unravel what all of this means. For how awful of a realization this is to me, if

this amount of time has gone by and nothing has come of
someone reading these contents then I feel that I must still go
ahead and make my way back to Bok. Right? Should I really let
this loom over me forever if I decided to run away again? What
is their angle? It would mean relentless and eternal puzzlement
if I did not find out more.

Everything seems fine. No reason to keep panicking.
Right? Make a choice and stick with it. There is still so much
mystery to that place that I need to learn about. I will take things
up with the horned Ernst immediately upon my return.

THE END

AND A
NEW BEGINNING
TO

NOTE:

I listened to Oingo Boingo every
single day while writing this book…

…and may do the same for the next.

Acknowledgement / Citation for Epigraph:

Not My Slave
Words and Music by Danny Elfman
Copyright © 1987 LITTLE MAESTRO MUSIC
All Rights Administered by SONGS OF UNIVERSAL, INC.
All Rights Reserved   Used by Permission
Reprinted by Permission of Hal Leonard LLC
Performed & Recorded by Oingo Boingo

9 798991 230230